Sully had alw

But Theresa was grateful he was here for her now.

"We'll get through this, Sully," she said, turning so she stood directly in front of him. She reached her arms up and locked her hands behind his neck. Gazing into his soot-colored eyes, she saw a spark of something she never thought she'd see again.

Beneath the worry, desire flared. He tightened his grip on her waist, tugging her closer to the solid warmth of his body.

She closed her eyes and leaned into him. In his arms again at last, she found the inner strength to believe that Eric would be returned to them, safe from harm.

"Theresa...we'll find him. We'll find our son and bring him home for Christmas."

ABOUT THE AUTHOR

Carla Cassidy is an award-winning author of more than forty books. She's been a cheerleader for the Kansas City Chiefs football team and has traveled the East Coast as a singer and dancer in a band. But the greatest pleasure she has had is in creating romance and happiness for readers. Carla lives in the Midwest with her husband, Frank.

Books by Carla Cassidy

HARLEQUIN INTRIGUE

379—PASSION IN THE FIRST DEGREE
411—SUNSET PROMISES*
415—MIDNIGHT WISHES*
419—SUNRISE VOWS*
*Cheyenne Nights miniseries

Their Only Child

Carla Cassidy

Harlequin Books

TORONTO • NEW YORK • LONDON
AMSTERDAM • PARIS • SYDNEY • HAMBURG
STOCKHOLM • ATHENS • TOKYO • MILAN
MADRID • WARSAW • BUDAPEST • AUCKLAND

To Pat Morris, talented writer and special friend. Thank you for being there to share the madness, the tears, and especially for possessing a special gift of laughter.

ISBN 0-373-22447-8

THEIR ONLY CHILD

This edition published by arrangement with Harlequin Books S.A.

Printed in U.S.A.

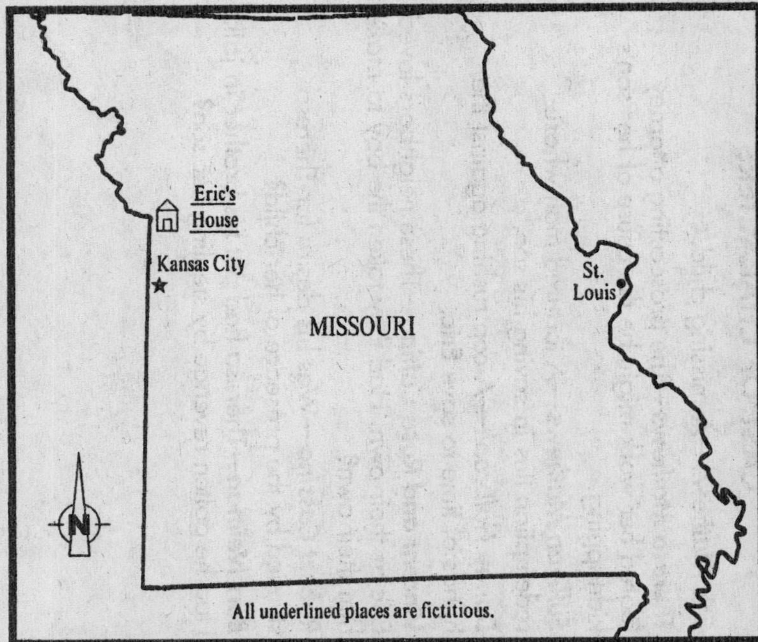

Eric's House
Kansas City
MISSOURI
St. Louis
N
All underlined places are fictitious.

CAST OF CHARACTERS

Eric Mathews—A missing child.

Theresa Mathews—The prosecuting attorney feared her work might be the cause of her son's kidnapping.

Sullivan Mathews—A tortured man whose redemption lies in saving his son.

Donny Holbrook—A cop rushing against the hands of time to save Eric.

Vincent and Rose Caltino—These neighbors loved Eric as their own. Had they taken the boy to *make* him their own?

Robert Cassino—Was his desire for Theresa stymied by the presence of her child?

Burt Neiman—Theresa had put his brother in jail. Had he gotten revenge by stealing her son?

Chapter One

December 22

Theresa Mathews glanced at the stove clock as she put the last dozen cookies into the oven. Three-thirty. Eric should be home from school in the next fifteen minutes or so.

She walked over to the table, where two dozen freshly baked cookies still awaited the layer of frosting and sprinkles that would change them from ordinary cookies to Christmas bells and trees.

She'd saved the decorating for Eric, although he'd never have confessed to his friends he liked to decorate cookies. Just as he didn't let on to them that he loved to read and needed a good-night kiss each night before he could sleep.

Theresa shook her head and smiled. Her little boy was shedding some of his childhood pieces, and she mourned the little boy gone, but anticipated the young man to come.

He'd be in a terrific mood today, given that it was the last day of school before the extended Christmas holiday. Three more days and Santa would arrive, bringing with him the computer game Eric had wanted, a new bicycle, and an official Joe Montana football jersey.

Of course, the one thing Eric wanted most for Christmas, she couldn't give him. She couldn't make them a family again. She shoved away thoughts of Sully, refusing to allow memories of her ex-husband to curtail her happy holiday spirit.

She was determined that this Christmas would be as wonderful as all Eric's past ones, despite the absence of his father.

"Yoo-hoo."

Theresa smiled when she heard the musical voice and the creak of the front door opening. "In the kitchen, Rose," she answered.

Rose appeared in the doorway between the living room and the kitchen, her broad face beaming a smile. "Where's my little guy?"

"Not home from school yet." Theresa motioned her next-door neighbor into a chair at the table. "You know Eric—the five-minute walk from school never takes him less than fifteen."

Rose set a gaily wrapped present next to her and reached for one of the cookies. "You can just slip this under the tree when you put the rest of the presents out," she said.

Theresa shook her head. "That's the third gift you've brought over for him. You're spoiling my son."

"Ah, how can you spoil a child like Eric?" Rose

popped a piece of the cookie into her mouth, then waved her hands dismissively. ''The sweetness of the saints was breathed into that boy.''

The moment Theresa and Eric moved into this house, ten months before, Rose Caltino and her husband, Vincent had adopted them. They treated Theresa as the child they'd never had, and had become indulgent, loving, surrogate grandparents to Eric.

''I saw in the paper this morning that you won your latest case,'' Rose said.

A flush of pleasure warmed Theresa's face. ''Yes. It looks like Roger Neiman will be enjoying the hospitality of prison for a long time to come.''

''The paper called you the rising star in the district attorney's office.''

Theresa laughed. ''Next week one of the other prosecutors will be the rising star. The paper likes whoever wins in the most recent case.''

''Maybe, but you're much better-looking than the other prosecutors,'' Rose exclaimed, making Theresa laugh once again.

''I think you might be prejudiced, my friend,'' she replied.

Rose grinned. ''Perhaps. And now I'd better get back home before Vincent comes looking for me. That man has been so mysterious lately, I'm beginning to think he has a girlfriend.''

Theresa laughed. Never had she seen a man so devoted to a woman as Vincent was to Rose. ''After thirty years of marriage, I don't think you have to worry about Vincent having a girlfriend. You two are the happiest couple I know."

Rose stood. "I'm a lucky woman. Anyway, I just wanted to bring that present by for Eric." Theresa walked with her through the living room to the front door. "When are you going to decorate the tree?" She gestured toward the perfectly formed Scotch pine in the stand in the corner.

"This evening. I'm going to make popcorn and hot spiced cider. If you and Vincent want to come over, you're welcome."

"We might just do that," Rose replied. Then, with a wave of her hand, she took off walking across the narrow swatch of lawn that separated her house from Theresa's.

Theresa watched her go, a warmth of affection sweeping through her as Rose turned one last time and waved. She was lucky to have neighbors like the Caltinos, lucky to have such special friends.

Looking at the clock once again, she frowned. Even if Eric stopped to examine every crack in the sidewalk, every crawling bug, he should have been home by now. Back in the kitchen, she placed lids over the frosting bowls, then grabbed her coat from the hall closet.

She went out the back door, breathing in the cold air that held the subtle scent of possible snow. She shoved her hands deep in her pockets. Snow would be nice. She was off work until after the holidays, and she wouldn't mind a bit if they were snowed in for a couple of days. It would be nice to have extra time to spend with Eric.

There were times when she suspected that on her days off Eric intentionally dawdled on his way home. It had become a common practice for her to come looking for him. When she found him, he shared with her whatever wonders had caused him to pause and linger.

Last week, it had been a leaf that resembled Abraham Lincoln's profile. The week before, it had been a spiderweb glistening in gossamer splendor in the boughs of a tree. Eric the explorer...that was what they'd called him from the moment he could walk. Never had Theresa seen a child who took more delight in the world around him.

As she walked down the tree-lined sidewalk, she once again congratulated herself on choosing to move to this tiny suburb, a mere half hour from downtown Kansas City.

Following their divorce, Sully had offered to move out of their midtown condo and let her and Eric remain, but she'd wanted something different, a new beginning. She'd needed someplace without painful memories, memories of laughter...and love.

As she moved down the sidewalk toward the elementary school, she scanned both sides of the street, looking for Eric. What had he worn to school that morning? She frowned, trying to remember. Jeans for sure. Since beginning the fourth grade, he wouldn't be caught dead in anything but jeans. A bright blue sweater, and his red Kansas City Chiefs coat. He should be easy to spot amid the browns of winter.

She reached the school building without spotting Eric. Maybe he'd had to stay after school, she thought. Although usually a good student, there were times his daydreaming got him into trouble. She smiled, her heart expanding with her love for the boy. God forbid a butterfly landed on the window during math class or an interestingly shaped cloud skittered by in the middle of social studies. Eric would be lost to a world where butterflies spoke and he could ride a cloud to the stars.

She frowned. Usually the teacher or the secretary called her when they were holding Eric after school. A small sense of disquiet stole through her as she headed for the school building.

The Kennedy Elementary School was a one-story brick building with a bike rack in front. The rack was empty, as was the hallway when Theresa walked inside. Again a tingle of vague nervousness raced up her spine. Her footsteps rang hollow against the shiny tiled floor as she walked down the long hallway.

She felt a surge of relief sweep through her when she saw the office lights still on. She walked in, and the secretary, Mrs. Jenkins, looked up and smiled. "Mrs. Mathews. What can I do for you?"

"I'm sorry to bother you. I'm looking for my errant son, and thought he might be here with you."

Mrs. Jenkins raised a hand to her lips. "Oh, goodness." She shuffled through some paperwork on her desk. "I think Eric was on the absentee list for today."

"Oh, no, that's impossible." A whisper of fear crawled up Theresa's throat, and she swallowed hard against it. "I didn't call him in sick, and nobody called me from the school."

"Oh, my, it's all my fault." Concern, mixed with apology, flickered in Mrs. Jenkins eyes. "I...I was in the middle of calling parents when Sammy Bowens came in with a bloody nose. The nurse was out of the building and I had to stop what I was doing and take care of him and, well, I guess I didn't get everyone called." She flicked through more papers, then picked up the one she sought. "Yes...here he is. Oh, God...I'm so sorry I didn't call you."

Theresa took the absentee list from her and scanned it, her gaze pausing on first her son's name, then another one. "I see Willie Simmons was absent, as well." She grasped a thread of hope. "I'll bet those two are together somewhere."

"Well, there you go." Mrs. Jenkins nodded her head in relief. "The two boys probably cooked up a day of playing hooky." She pushed her phone toward Theresa. "Why don't you call Mrs. Simmons? I imagine you'll find that she doesn't know anything about Willie missing school today, either."

Theresa quickly punched in the numbers to Willie's house, hoping, praying the boys would be there, getting a sound lecture from Mrs. Simmons. One ring. Two rings. She listened to ten rings before she replaced the phone in its cradle. "No answer," she said.

"Perhaps Mrs. Simmons is out looking for the boys, or she could be on her way to your house with Eric."

"Yes...yes, I'm sure you're right." Theresa felt a nervous tic pulsing in the side of her neck. "I'd better get right home."

"I'm sure it will be okay," Mrs. Jenkins said, although Theresa heard the concern in the older woman's voice. "Eric and Willie aren't the first little boys to decide they need a day off from the classroom."

Surely Mrs. Jenkins was right, Theresa thought as she hurried out of the building and down the sidewalk toward home.

Surely the boys had just decided to play hooky. It wouldn't be the first time Willie and Eric had made a poor choice that led them into trouble. Both boys were bright, but somehow, when they got together, they only functioned on half a brain between them.

I'll ground him for a month, she vowed, her footsteps a rapid staccato on the sidewalk. *I'll take away his computer privileges. I'll make him do the dishes for the next six weeks.*

She focused all her thoughts on punishment, refusing to think of any other scenario than that the two boys had skipped school and were probably hiding out someplace in fear of the consequences of their actions.

"Eric?" she called out the moment she reentered

the house. No answer...and no sign that he'd been home.

Don't panic, she instructed herself calmly as the pulse in her neck throbbed in an unsteady rhythm. Boys, in the irresponsibility of youth and the pursuit of adventure, often lost track of time, not thinking of worried adults.

She went to the phone and punched in Willie's number once again. She nearly sobbed in relief when the phone was answered on the third ring and she recognized Willie's voice.

"Willie, this is Eric's mother. Is Eric there with you?"

"No. We've been gone to the doctor's office. I got the measles."

"Is that why you weren't in school today?" Theresa tightened her grip on the phone cord.

"Yup, I woke up all spotty and Mom kept me home."

"So, you haven't seen Eric all day?" Theresa's voice was weak, thready, and the blood pounded loudly in her ears.

"I talked to him on the phone last night, but I haven't talked to him since then."

"When you spoke to him last night, did he say anything about visiting any other friends...? Did he mention special plans for today?"

There was a long pause...a pause Theresa wanted to fill with a scream. Instead, she swallowed the scream and twisted the phone cord more tightly around her hand. "Please, Willie...try to think where he might be."

"Well, Bobby Michaels's dog had puppies yesterday, and Eric really wanted to see them."

"Thank you, Willie. If you see or hear from Eric, would you tell him to call me right away?" Theresa hung up the phone, fighting down a nauseating fear that threatened to overwhelm her.

She immediately pulled her personal phone book out of the drawer and began calling the numbers of Eric's friends, beginning with Bobby Michaels.

By the time she'd phoned everyone she could think of her fear was a living, breathing entity inside her, threatening to suffocate her. Nobody. Nobody had seen or heard from Eric all day long.

"Where is he?" she breathed aloud. She sank down at the kitchen table and stared at the cookies, awaiting their festive holiday dress. Where was her baby? Where was Eric?

She thought of phoning Sully, but knew it was pointless. If by some minor miracle Eric had managed to get to his father's apartment, Sully would have immediately called her. Nor would Sully have made plans to spend the day with Eric without okaying it with her first. Sully didn't function that way.

She picked up the phone one last time, and quickly punched the numbers *911*, her entire body trembling as the realization struck her full force. Eric was not just an hour late coming home from school. He'd been missing for over nine hours.

THE SOUND pierced through the stillness of the apartment. Sullivan Mathews flailed his arms and backhanded his clock radio to ward off the discordant sound. The radio crashed to the floor, and he burrowed his head deeper into the pillows.

When the annoying noise came again, he realized it wasn't the clock, it was the phone. Rolling over on his back without opening his eyes, he grabbed the receiver and held it to his ear.

"Sully...are you there?" Kip Pearson's voice boomed over the line, and Sully swallowed a growl of displeasure.

"I just went to bed," he exclaimed as he reached down to the floor for the alarm clock. The digital numbers told him it was almost 5:00 p.m. "Correction, I've been in bed for exactly one hour." He rolled over on his back, feeling the last vestiges of sleep disappearing.

He should have known better than to spend the morning in the gym. He'd finally gotten away from the club at five that morning, and he should have come home and gone directly to bed. Instead, he'd spent the day working out, then had eaten an obscenely large dinner to make up for all the exercise. He scrubbed a hand over his face. "What's up?" he asked his friend.

"We just got word of a 911 call."

Sully frowned. "So? It's not like I'm on the force anymore. Why should I care about a 911 call?"

There was a long pause. "Sully...it was from your ex-wife."

Sully shot up to a sitting position, the phone receiver pressed painfully against his ear. "What?"

"Sully...your kid is missing. He's been missing since early this morning."

Sully didn't hear any more. He slammed down the receiver and shot from the bed. Eric missing? There had to be a mistake. He grabbed a pair of jeans and a shirt.

As he dressed, a million thoughts raced through his head. Remain calm, he instructed himself. There was probably a logical explanation. Lots of kids lost track of time, especially kids like Eric.

He grabbed his wallet and car keys, but before leaving he paused in the living room, next to a large wire pen. Inside the pen, a collie puppy looked at him with soulful brown eyes. Eric's Christmas present. Theresa would probably kill him, but he'd decided the kid needed a dog. And if his ex-wife threw too big a fit, Sully figured, the dog could stay here for Eric's semimonthly visits.

He placed a handful of dry food in the cage, gave the pooch a pat on the head, then raced out the door, trying to hold on to his calm until he knew exactly what was going on.

ERIC FIRST BECAME AWARE of the feel of an unfamiliar, thin mattress beneath his body. He was lying on his stomach, and the odor of the mattress was damp and sour. His nostrils flared at the unpleasant scent. He swiped at his mouth, embarrassed to discover he'd been drooling.

It was dark...the darkest dark he'd ever seen. In his room at home, even when his mom turned out his lamp on the table next to his bed, light still spilled in from the window...moonlight, the glow from the street lamp, the pinpoint of illumination from his night-light. No matter how dark it got...it never got this dark.

He rolled over on his back, groaning as a headache tried to take off the top of his head. Where was he? What had happened? He frowned, trying to remember. It was hard to think. His brain seemed mushed all together in his skull. He worked his mouth open and closed. He felt as though it had been stuffed with cotton. Was he sick? No...that didn't seem right.

He remembered eating cereal for breakfast. He remembered walking to school. It had been a pretty day. The sky had been a perfect shade of blue, like a crayon that was fresh and sharp. He'd seen a leaf that looked like a galloping horse. A bird had chattered to him from the high branch of a tree. Then...

He squeezed his eyes tightly closed, trying to remember, needing to remember. Hands grabbing him from behind...strong arms pulling him...something sickly-sweet-smelling pressed against his nose and mouth...then a wave of cold and nothing.

He wanted to yell for help, but was afraid to. It smelled bad, kind of like Rose's basement, where she had shelves of fruit and vegetables in jars and potatoes and onions in big, wooden bins.

It's a dream, he reasoned. *Sooner or later I'll wake up and be in my own bedroom and Mom will be frying bacon and hollering to me to get out of bed and clean my room or Santa Claus won't come.*

He'd had bad dreams before. He squeezed his eyes tightly closed. All he had to do was wait for night to pass, then he'd wake up in his own bed. He'd tell his mom all about this crazy, scary dream, and they'd laugh about it. Keeping his eyes tightly closed, Eric waited for his nightmare to pass.

Chapter Two

Theresa paced the floor of the living room as she answered the questions Officer Donny Holbrook asked. With every question that was repeated, she was aware of time passing.

She'd been grateful to see Donny Holbrook's familiar, handsome face at her door a few minutes earlier. Donny had been Sully's partner on the force before Sully resigned, and Donny had been an occasional visitor to their home when she and Sully were still married.

"And so the last time you saw him was this morning when he left for school?" Donny sat on the edge of the sofa, a notebook and pen in his hand.

"Yes." Theresa sighed. "Donny, we've gone over this a dozen times already. No, Eric wasn't angry or upset about anything. He wouldn't have just run away." She stared in frustration at the middle-aged, blond-haired cop. *Why was he sitting there so calmly? Why wasn't he out there, doing something, anything, to find her little boy?*

"Is it possible he went to see Sully?" Donny asked. "Has he been upset about the divorce?"

Theresa sat down on the chair across from the police sergeant. "Of course Eric was upset about the divorce, but he's adjusting. And no, he wouldn't have gone to see Sully without permission. Besides, Sully lives miles from here. Eric wouldn't attempt getting there on his own. And if he had, Sully would have called me."

"We have somebody trying to get hold of Sully now," Donny replied. "Problems in school?"

"No, no more than the usual kid stuff." Theresa squeezed her eyes closed, refusing to allow tears to fall, even though they burned hot behind her eyelids.

"Would he have gotten into somebody's car, perhaps a stranger's?"

Theresa shook her head. "Absolutely not. He wouldn't have gotten into an acquaintance's car, either. Eric and I have a password, and if the person doesn't know the password, then Eric won't go with them."

"Smart." Donny nodded in approval, then stood. "Do you mind if I have a look around in his room?" He smiled sympathetically. "Theresa, you know there are certain procedures that have to be followed."

She nodded and pointed down the hallway. "First door on the left."

As he disappeared in the direction of the bedroom, Theresa walked into the kitchen. She didn't want to hear about procedures. She was tired of questions. She wanted somebody to find Eric—now.

Where was he? Where could he be? She tasted her fear, felt hysteria only a breath away. But she refused to give in to it, afraid that if she allowed her fear to take over, she'd lose her mind.

The refrigerator motor kicked on, humming into the relative silence of the house. Normal sounds, for normal times. She could hear the muted sounds of Donny in the bedroom, and if she closed her eyes, she could almost imagine it was Eric playing in his room and all was right with the world.

She went to the window and looked out, somehow feeling that if she stared long enough she'd see Eric coming down the street, hurrying because he knew he was in big trouble.

He'd have a wonderful story about a caterpillar he'd captured, or a bird who'd beckoned him to follow her to an old nest. Theresa wouldn't care where he'd been. She wouldn't care what he'd done. As long as he was safe.

The front door opened, and her heart jumped into her throat with hope. "Eric?" she called, and ran into the living room.

Her ex-husband stood in the doorway. Clad in worn, tight blue jeans and a wrinkled cotton shirt, for a moment he didn't say a word. He simply held out his arms to her.

Suddenly she was in his embrace, being held tightly against his body warmth, his broad chest, with his familiar scent filling her head.

The tears she'd held in check for the past several hours flowed freely as she buried her face against the curve of his neck, needing to be near the only person in the world who must be feeling the same fear, the same bewilderment, the same horrendous loss she felt.

His arms enfolded her, his hands stroking down the length of her hair. "It's all right, Theresa. I'm sure it will be all right." And somehow, at the strong assurance in his voice, she believed it, for just a moment.

"How did you know?" she asked, not moving from his embrace.

"Kip heard about the 911 call. He phoned me and I came right over."

She stirred from his arms when she heard Donny leaving Eric's bedroom. He entered the living room, and he and Sully nodded to each other.

"So, what's the story?" Sully asked.

As Donny filled in Sully, Theresa sank onto the sofa. It was crazy. There had been a time when she was madly in love with Sully, then a time when she was incredibly angry with him. Most recently, she'd simply tried to put him out of her life, out of her thoughts.

Yes, it was crazy, but she was glad he was here. She knew Sully would demand action, and if by sheer willpower alone he could find Eric, he would.

She'd seen little of him since their divorce, and as he listened intently to what Donny told him, she looked at him, noting the changes the past months had wrought in him.

Sullivan Mathews had always been a big man. Standing over six feet, he'd been built like a football player, with massive shoulders and slender hips. He'd lost weight, Theresa observed. Although his shoulders appeared just as broad, he'd lost any hint of a protruding gut, and his face seemed thinner, older.

Still, with his gunmetal-colored eyes and dark hair, he was an attractive man. His features were hard, unforgiving, and yet she knew that when he smiled, his face lit with a character and charisma that had once made him a favorite target for newspaper articles and photos.

"Have you started canvassing the area?" he asked Donny.

Donny nodded. "We've got men out between here and your son's school. We're also checking with all the hospitals in the area."

Sully nodded, as if satisfied for the moment that everything that could be done was being done. "You called all his friends?" he asked Theresa.

She nodded, her fingers lacing and unlacing in her lap. "None of them have seen or heard from him today."

"I think we have to face the possibility that Eric might have been kidnapped," Donny said.

"Kidnapped?" Theresa looked at him blankly, the word not having a place in her reality, in her comprehension. "But...why? Why would somebody want to kidnap him?'' She looked at Sully, willing him to deny the possibility.

''If it is a kidnapping, then we should hear something about a ransom soon,'' Sully said. ''But it's a little early for us to jump to that conclusion.''

Donny nodded his agreement. Sully then looked at Theresa. ''Would you mind making a pot of coffee? It's cold outside, and as the officers check in here, I'm sure they'd appreciate a cup.''

''Of course.'' She jumped up, eager for the activity, any activity, to occupy her.

She went into the kitchen and got out a serving tray, along with mugs, the sugar bowl and the creamer. Noticing that the sugar bowl was nearly empty, she opened the cabinet and grabbed the sack of sugar, pausing when she saw the boxes of cereal lined up side by side.

The colorful box of Trix stared at her. *Trix are for kids*...and they were Eric's favorite. But this morning he'd wanted pancakes.

''Please, Mom? Please, please make me pancakes,'' he'd begged, smiling impishly. ''I'll give you ten kisses if you do.''

She captured the memory in her mind, savored it like a piece of sweet chocolate in her mouth. He'd come to the breakfast table talking about Wendy Sorrie's broken arm and the cast she'd let everyone sign the day before.

She'd barely listened to his chatter, preoccupied with all the things she needed to do before Christmas morning. There were still gifts to be wrapped, and she'd promised to make homemade divinity for the church party.

"Ten kisses, Mom," he'd said again, playfully, trying to bribe her.

She'd set the box of cereal and the carton of milk in front of him. "How about one kiss and a bowl of Trix?" She'd kissed him soundly on the forehead, then gone back to making out her grocery list.

Her hand shook as she took the box of cereal down from the cabinet. She hugged it to her chest, almost able to feel the warmth of his fingers lingering on the cardboard as he poured a bowlful only that morning. His fingers...long and slender, always with dirty nails from his digging and exploring.

She closed her eyes, remembering the scent of his hair, the sweet brush of his lips against her cheek as he'd kissed her goodbye. Her chest ached with the need to reverse the hours, stop time, grab hold of him and not allow him to walk out that front door.

"Theresa?"

She spun around to see Sully standing hesitantly in the doorway. She opened her mouth, then closed it, unable to speak for a moment.

She held out the box of cereal, her vision blurring with the burden of tears. "He wanted pancakes this morning." She dropped the box to the floor, a sobbing gasp caught in her throat. "I didn't make them for him. I gave him cereal."

In three long strides, Sully reached her. He smelled of minty soap and winter winds and the familiar scent that was simply Sully. His body seemed to surround her, his musculature comforting in its very solidness. "Theresa, you can't fall apart now. You've always been so strong. You need to be strong now."

She moved out of his arms, his words vaguely irritating. "Why can't I fall apart? When things got tough before, that's exactly what you did."

He stepped backward, as if she'd physically punched him.

"I'm sorry, Sully," she whispered, horrified by what she'd allowed herself to say. "I shouldn't have said that. I'm just so scared."

"I know." He shoved his hands in his pockets, a familiar gesture that let her know he was as worried as she. "Donny wants to know if you have a recent photo of Eric, something he can get copied. The pictures I have are out-of-date."

Theresa nodded and went to the kitchen desk drawer. "We just got his school pictures last week." She removed an envelope from the drawer and withdrew the contents. "Eric was going to frame one of the eight-by-tens as one of your Christmas presents." She handed him one of the smaller photos. "Sully...do you really think Eric has been kidnapped?"

He thrust a hand through his thick, dark hair. "I don't know, Theresa. I don't know what to think. Eric's a good kid. If he could come home, he'd be here." He looked at her, his gray eyes dark with the torture of his thoughts. "I think it's a possibility, but at this point everything is a possibility."

Theresa's heart ached as if icy hands were clutching it tight, cutting off blood. "I'm so afraid," she whispered.

He hesitated a moment. "It's going to be all right," he said, as if to reassure himself as much as her.

They looked at each other, and somewhere in the back of her mind, Theresa wondered how they had messed up so badly, how they had lost each other in the past two years.

They both froze as the phone rang.

In an instant, Sully grabbed her and pulled her into the living room where Donny was about to pick up the phone. "Don't." The single word shot out of him like a bullet. "Let her answer it." He motioned to Theresa.

"We don't have any equipment hooked in yet," Donny replied. "We won't be able to trace."

"She still needs to answer it," Sully replied, and nodded to Theresa.

Theresa felt as if she'd swallowed a cotton swab. Her mouth was achingly dry. *Let it be Eric,* she prayed. She wanted it to be him, saying he was lost, assuring her he was fine, just scared and embarrassed.

Sully moved to her side and pointed to the phone. Wiping her sweaty palms down the side of her slacks, she drew a deep breath, then snatched up the receiver. "Hello?" Sully pressed his face against hers, sharing the call.

"Mrs. Mathews? This is Mrs. Jenkins."

Theresa expelled her breath and closed her eyes in despair. "The school secretary," she whispered. "Yes, Mrs. Jenkins. No, no, we haven't heard from him yet. The police are here now." Theresa answered the woman's questions, thanked her for the call, then hung up the phone.

"Now what do we do?" she whispered bleakly.

"We wait," Sully said. "All we can do is wait."

SULLY had never been a patient man, and waiting for something to happen, for some information to surface, had always been a part of police work that he hated. Now that it was his own kid that was missing, the waiting was the worst kind of torture he'd ever known.

As Theresa paced the kitchen floor, and Donny coordinated the neighborhood search efforts, Sully drifted down the hallway and into Eric's bedroom.

He hadn't been inside the house before tonight, had respected Theresa's privacy and her need to establish a home separate from him.

Every other weekend, he pulled up out front and Eric ran out to his car for their weekend visits. Now he wanted...needed...to see the place where his son lived and dreamed, the place he slept each night.

Eric's room. It breathed with the essence of the little boy. It held the scent of hidden cookies, cedar chips and childhood dreams.

The bed was covered with a brown-and-blue plaid spread, haphazardly pulled up and crooked on one side. Obviously, Eric had made it himself that morning.

The walls were decorated with posters of the Kansas City Chiefs football players, one wall exclusively dedicated to the retired quarterback Joe Montana...Eric's hero.

A hamster cage sat on the nightstand, a small sign propped in front of it. *My friend Petey* was scrawled in bright red crayon. At the moment, the white hamster slept in a pile of cedar shavings, unaware that his friend Eric might be in trouble.

Sully sat on the edge of the bed and reached down to get a stuffed rabbit that peeked out at him from beneath it. The bunny was white, missing an eye, and with an ear that dangled from a remaining piece of thread.

He and Theresa had bought it for Eric for his second Easter. Eric had adored the stuffed animal, carried it with him everywhere, and refused to fall asleep at night unless Bunny was next to him in bed.

A night-light burned in the socket against one wall, the eternal light of little boys and girls everywhere, with the magic to keep monsters away.

Eric was a boy full of incongruities. A boy who was fascinated with the rough-and-tumble world of football, yet who needed a night-light burning in the night. On top of the dresser was a collection of odds and ends, leaves, nutshells, pinecones, a congregation of nature in the church that was boyhood. An explorer who still slept with his favorite stuffed animal in his arms.

Sully gripped the bunny against his chest for a moment, wishing the rabbit could tell him his son's last thoughts, any secrets Eric might have had that would let Sully know where he might be. With a sigh, Sully pushed the bunny back under the bed, knowing his son would want the childish bedtime companion to remain his secret.

Dusk was falling...and soon after that, night would come. Night, with its darkness. Night, with its lurking shadows and hidden secrets. He had to do something. He couldn't just sit around any longer.

He left Eric's room, pulled his coat on and started for the front door, stopping only when Theresa called his name.

"What are you doing?" she asked.

"I can't stand around here doing nothing. I'm going to go out and look for him."

"Wait." She opened the hall-closet door. "I'll come with you."

"No. You have to stay here." His heart ached as he recognized the tension that made her face pale and drawn.

"But, I need to come...I need to do something," she protested.

He placed his hands on her shoulders, as always amazed by how tiny she was physically, knowing how strong she was emotionally. "Theresa, you have to stay here, in case we get a phone call. Your place is here."

"Of course." She nodded. "You're right." She reached into the closet and pulled out a plaid muffler.

Reaching up on tiptoe, she wound the cotton material around the collar of his jacket. "Stay warm."

He nodded, touched by her concern, then stepped outside into the cold night air. Cold. And growing darker. And Eric wasn't home.

Instead of taking his car, he opted to walk the same route Eric would have taken that morning to go to school. He walked slowly, methodically, his gaze inching intently over not only the sidewalk, but the yards on either side of the road, as well.

When he was a rookie on the police department, he'd worked a missing-kid case. The five-year-old girl had finally been found, unharmed but frightened, her foot helplessly twisted in a tangle of roots in a drainage ditch.

He hoped that was what had happened to Eric. That somehow he'd fallen into a hole, gotten tangled in a vine, slipped into a ditch, and would be found safe. But Sully had a bad feeling in his gut...the instincts of a cop.

It seemed somehow obscene for him to be walking in the cold, his heart aching for his missing son, while on the houses he passed Christmas lights blinked and raced in festive, kaleidoscopic fashion.

An illuminated plastic Santa Claus waved to him from a front porch, and a reindeer danced on top of a roof, a brilliant red nose piercing the falling darkness of night.

Where was Eric? He should be home, getting ready for bed and dreams of Santa Claus and presents.

Sully reached the school building, now dark and empty. He pulled the muffler closer around his neck, the cold seeping inside him, wrapping around his heart. Where was Eric?

He looked at his watch, surprised to find it had taken him an hour to walk the five-minute course from Theresa's house to the school. He turned to head back, again walking slowly, pausing to check out every ditch, open garage and shed he passed along the way. He was halfway home when he saw Kip Pearson approaching.

"Theresa told me you were out here," Kip said as he fell into step beside Sully. "I thought I'd come by and see what I could do to help."

"Thanks, Kip, although I'm not sure at this point what anyone can do." Still, Sully was touched by Kip's appearance. He knew Kip had probably just finished a full shift at the station and had his own family waiting for him at home.

"So, there's been no news?" Kip asked.

Sully shook his head. "Nothing. It's like Eric walked off the face of the earth."

"Who caught the case?"

"Donny Holbrook." Sully replied as he jammed his hands in his pockets.

"He's a good cop," Kip replied. He cast a sideways look at Sully. "You can't blame him for what happened that night."

Sully knew exactly what night Kip referred to...the night his life had shattered. The night he'd stopped being a cop, stopped being a husband, and instead become a self-destructive drunk. "I don't. Emotionally, I'm still angry about the whole incident, but I don't know who to blame."

"I hear you've been on the wagon."

Sully nodded. "Six months clean and sober."

"Thought about coming back to the department? You know they'd love to get you back on the force. You were a damned good cop, Sully."

Sully didn't reply. A day didn't go by that he didn't think about going back into the department. But he couldn't...wouldn't...go back until somebody on the police force addressed the fact that Sully believed he'd been set up by a fellow cop.

And deep inside, he feared there was another reason he couldn't go back to the force, a reason he'd never spoken aloud to anyone...a reason that gave him nightmares every night of his life.

He shoved these thoughts aside. He had more important things to worry about at the moment. "Eric never showed up at school this morning," he said to Kip. "He walked out of the house and just disappeared."

Theresa's house came into view, and Sully slowed his footsteps, wishing he had some news to tell his ex-wife, wishing he was holding Eric in his arms.

"Holbrook thinks there's a possibility Eric's been kidnapped," he said.

"I suppose nobody can rule that out, especially with Theresa just coming off such a controversial, high-profile case."

They both paused as they stepped onto the front porch. ''So, what do you think?'' Kip asked.

Sully shoved his hands into his coat pocket. Yes, kidnapping was a possibility, one he didn't want to consider. The thought of somebody intentionally holding his son, away from his home, from the parents who loved him, sent frigid chills racing up his spine. "I think I've never been so cold in my life. Come on, let's go inside and get some hot coffee.''

Chapter Three

Night fell slowly, inch by inch, dark clouds spilling ominously across the sky to steal the last of the day's light. The appearance of the darkness filled Theresa with a new kind of anguish.

Eric didn't like the dark. From the time he was a baby, he'd been afraid of the dark. He'd always had a night-light burning in his room. And now he was someplace out there...in the darkness...alone.

And it was cold. The forecast was for snow. Was he someplace warm? The thought of her baby out there in the dark, in the cold, had the capacity to drive her mad if she allowed it.

As Theresa stared out the kitchen window, she was vaguely aware of activity behind her. The coffeepot gurgled with a fresh brew, and police officers drifted in and out of the kitchen, getting warm and drinking coffee before returning to the cold, dark night and the seeming futility of their search.

Hours had passed since she called the police, hours of men pounding sidewalks, checking drainage ditches, investigating any place where a little boy might hide or could have fallen. Nothing. It was as if the earth itself had opened up and swallowed Eric without a trace.

Theresa had never been so frightened. She'd been hurt when her marriage died, afraid when Sully finally made the decision to leave her. At that time, a year ago, she'd been deathly scared of facing life alone, starting her life anew. But that fear couldn't even begin to touch the terror that gripped her now.

A burst of laughter broke through her thoughts. She glanced behind her to the table, where three policemen were teasing a fourth. Their laughter sounded again, melodic and rich.

Although she knew it was irrational, she wanted to scream at them to stop laughing. Laughter didn't belong here, not when Eric wasn't home. Instead, she bit the sides of her cheeks, knowing that the last thing she wanted to do was alienate the very men who were trying to help.

"Theresa?"

She turned at the sound of Donny's deep voice. He held out a cup of coffee. "Here, why don't you take this? It looks like it's going to be a long night." His voice was kind, filled with sympathy.

She forced a grateful smile and took the cup from him. "Thanks." As the other officers left the kitchen, Theresa sank into one of their vacated seats at the table.

Donny joined her, sitting across from her. "We need to talk."

"About Eric?"

Donny shook his head. "About Sully."

Theresa frowned. "What about him? Surely you don't believe he had anything to do with Eric's disappearance?"

"No, no, nothing like that." Donny got up and poured himself a cup of coffee, then rejoined her at the table. "I know Sullivan Mathews probably just about as well as anyone, and I know he loves his kid. He'd never do anything like this."

"Then what do you want to know about him?" Theresa asked. She wrapped her fingers around her cup, seeking the warmth to chase away the chill that had invaded her body.

"I've heard through the grapevine that he's working as a bouncer in some dive."

"He's a bouncer at Sam's Pit, over on Proctor Street."

"Rough area," Donny observed.

Theresa nodded. "I suppose." Not only was the neighborhood surrounding Sam's Pit known to be a rough area, but the bar itself was a known trouble spot, where fights broke out often and police presence was a nightly necessity.

"Does Sully talk about his work to you? Has he mentioned having problems with anyone in particular at the bar?"

Theresa bit back a burst of bitter laughter. "Sullivan hasn't talked to me in a very long time, Donny. Since the divorce, we rarely talk at all, unless it has something to do with Eric."

"Yeah." Donny frowned. "I guess he pretty much stopped talking to everyone after that night."

That night. Theresa knew exactly what night Donny spoke of...the night that had begun the end of her marriage, the night Sully had been shot.

Theresa saw the pain reflected in Donny's eyes, knew the self-recriminations he must have suffered as Sully's partner. She touched his hand lightly. "Don't blame yourself, Donny. I don't blame you, and I know Sully doesn't, either. You couldn't help it that you were sick. It was just one of those crazy quirks of fate."

"But I should have been there, watching his back." Donny's voice filled with pain. "That was my job, and I let him down."

Theresa sighed tiredly. "Nobody let Sully down except Sully." She pushed away thoughts of the past, not wanting to expend any energy on what couldn't be changed. "And if you want to find out about Sully's work now, you'll have to ask him."

Donny nodded and took a sip of his coffee, as if he needed a moment to push the past away. "What about your work?" he said a moment later. "Made anybody really mad at you lately?"

"Donny, I'm a prosecuting attorney—I'm always making people mad at me," she replied dryly.

"Maybe you should start making a list of names." He tore a sheet of paper off his note pad and handed it to her, along with a pen.

Theresa stared down at the sheet of paper, then

looked back at Donny. "You really think Eric has been kidnapped?"

"I think we need to consider it a definite possibility," Donny replied.

"But why haven't we received a call...a note? And why Eric? We aren't wealthy people," she protested, trying to make sense of the senseless.

Donny looked around. "You appear to be doing all right. Your picture is sometimes in the paper. To some people, that equates money. Besides, this might not be about money. Maybe it's about revenge."

Theresa swallowed hard. The idea of somebody taking Eric, keeping him away from her and Sully for revenge, horrified her. "Oh, Donny, I've prosecuted more than a hundred cases over my career. I...I don't even know where to begin."

"Concentrate on your cases over the last six months. Try to think of anyone who might want to get back at you, somebody who might have made threats." Donny drained his coffee, then stood. "I've got to get back to my men. I'll check with you for that list in a little while."

When he'd left the kitchen, Theresa once again looked down at the paper. It was a daunting task, to remember all the threats she'd received from all the people she was instrumental in putting behind bars.

She got up from the table and left the kitchen, knowing that in order to do a proper job, she needed to be in her office, where she kept files from all her cases.

The tiny third bedroom served as an at-home office. She preferred to spend the evening hours with Eric, and as a result she often burned the midnight oil, working in here, after Eric went to bed.

Grateful for something, anything, constructive to do that might help find Eric, she turned on her computer and pulled up a list of files.

As one of the lead prosecutors in the district attorney's office, Theresa worked the more heinous crime cases. Daily she faced off against the dregs of society, and the thought that one of those people might have her little boy filled her with cold, gut-wrenching terror.

Idle threats, spit out in the heat of conviction, were common in her cases. The bailiffs often joked that their jobs were secure as long as Theresa Mathews continued to work in the prosecutor's office.

She started searching her files for cases that had occurred six months before, deciding to work forward in time. She checked not only the cases she'd won, but those she'd lost, as well, trying to remember a face, a name, of anyone who'd seemed particularly filled with malevolence toward her.

Her gaze went often to the window, where the night had deepened to a darkness so profound it ached inside her. Each moment that passed, her heart cried out for Eric.

She had sifted through the first three months of cases and had a list of ten names when she stopped and stretched with arms overhead to work a kink out of her neck.

Her eyes felt grainy with suppressed emotion, and

she wondered if she'd ever be warm again. The chill inside her seemed to reach clear to her soul.

Scooting some papers aside on the top of her desk, her heart seemed to stop as she uncovered a drawing done in brilliant crayons. The picture depicted a fireplace, with three stockings hung above a cozy fire. On one stocking was carefully written *Eric*...the others said *Mom* and *Dad.* A plate of carefully drawn Oreo cookies and a glass of milk sat on the hearth. Across the top of the picture Eric had written a note in his boyish scrawl.

Don't forget the cookies for Santa. I love you, Mom.

She clutched it to her chest, her hand trembling uncontrollably. He must have drawn it the night before and snuck it in here some time this morning, before leaving for school. He often drew her pictures and left them on her desk to be discovered at some point in the day.

Tears burned, splashing hot on her cheeks. She tried to stop them, knew she had to remain strong, in control.

She couldn't cry for Eric. To cry for him meant something bad had happened...and she couldn't allow herself to think that...mustn't allow it.

Carefully she uncrumpled the picture, running her hands over and over it to take out any wrinkles. Then, just as carefully, she folded it in half, then in half again, until it was small enough to fit in her breast pocket...the pocket that covered her heart.

Swiping at her tears, she focused once again on her computer screen, hoping...praying...Eric would be found, safe and well before she finished making her list.

ONCE BACK AT THE HOUSE, Sully and Kip met Donny at the door. Donny shook his head in answer to the unspoken question in Sully's eyes. "Where's Theresa?" Sully asked.

"In her office, making me a list of people who might want to harm her," Donny explained. "You might want to do the same thing."

Sullivan nodded. He knew Donny was right. Having them make out a list of people who might want to cause them pain was the next logical step in the inquiry into Eric's disappearance. Eventually, he and Theresa would be asked to submit to a lie-detector test as part of the ongoing investigation.

He was beginning to hope for a ransom demand, to hope that Eric's disappearance was a real kidnapping and not a stranger abduction. It was rare that stranger abductions were ever solved—and rare that the children of such senseless crimes were returned to their parents alive....

A nauseating churning attacked his stomach as he thought of his son. Despite the divorce, in spite of Sully's personal demons...demons that had resulted in the breakup of his marriage...he and Eric had maintained a bond of closeness most fathers would envy.

The thought of Eric being afraid...cold... harmed...filled Sully with a grief too deep to maintain, a rage too overwhelming to entertain.

He started down the hallway, wanting to talk to Theresa. He met her as she barreled out of the back bedroom and collided with him.

"Sully." She gripped his arms, her fingers tight, her eyes burning with fierce determination. "We need to go to county lockup."

"What?" He looked at her in surprise. He'd once believed she was the most beautiful woman in the Midwest. Even now, with her blue eyes fevered, her face as pale as chalk and her dark hair a tangled mess, she looked beautiful.

Regret surged through him. If he and Theresa had stayed together, would Eric be missing now? If Sully hadn't fallen apart, started drinking and decided his wife and child were better off without him, would this all be happening?

There was no easy answer, and in any case it didn't matter. Sully was a failure, a screwup, and this woman had no place in what life he'd made for himself. What mattered now was Eric. "Why the county lockup?" he asked as Theresa attempted to push past him. "Theresa?" He grabbed her by the shoulders. "What's at the county lockup?"

"Roger Neiman. God, I don't know why I didn't think of him before now."

"Who's Roger Neiman?"

"A young man who was convicted two days ago for drug trafficking. A man who made all kinds of personal threats toward me when he was being led out of the courtroom."

"Theresa..." As she struggled to free herself from his grasp, he tightened his grip on her shoulders. She looked frantic, more out of control than he'd ever seen her. She'd always been so in control, the strong one. "Think about it. If this Roger is in jail, then he can't have Eric."

"That's true, but he might know something. He has a brother on the outside to carry out his threats. Oh, Sully, don't you see? We have to check it out. We have to."

Sully looked at her and recognized the tight leash she held on her self-control. A nerve ticked at the corner of one of her eyes, and her lower lip quivered, making her look more vulnerable than Sully had ever seen. "Okay, let's go talk to Donny."

Not long after, Sully, Theresa and Donny were in Donny's unmarked car, heading for the county jail. Donny had tried to insist that Sully and Theresa remain at the house while he went to the jail and questioned Roger, but Theresa would have none of that. She'd insisted she be the one to question Roger, and finally Donny had agreed.

When they left, an officer had been working on the phone line, setting up a tracer and recording equipment. Kip had offered to take phone duty until they returned. Sully knew Donny had pulled some strings in order to get the phones tapped so quickly. Without a ransom note, without a definite finger pointing to a kidnapping, such action would normally take longer than a mere ten or twelve hours.

The ride was accomplished in silence. Theresa stared intently out the window, as if by sheer willpower she might be able to conjure Eric out of the darkness of the night.

Sully wanted to take her hand, assure her everything would be all right, but he knew better than to offer Theresa meaningless platitudes. And in any case, he'd lost the right to hold her hand a year before, when he walked out of her life.

He leaned his head back against the seat, exhaustion tugging at him, but too emotionally strung to even consider sleep. He thought about Donny's suggestion earlier, that he think of anyone who might want to harm him.

Rubbing his chest, through his shirt he felt the puckered scar that was a physical reminder of the night he'd almost died. A day hadn't gone by since the shooting eighteen months ago that he didn't consider who might want to harm him.

He closed his eyes, thinking of that night. It was a night much like this one...dark, the moon and stars obscured by thick clouds. Although, on that night, it had been hot, a June night, unnaturally humid and stifling.

Sully had gotten word that one of his street snitches wanted to talk to him. Even though Donny had gone home sick with the flu and Sully knew that it was unwise to set up a meet without backup, he'd done just that.

The snitch, Louie Albright, was a street punk who'd come up with valuable information from time to time. Sully was working a difficult burglary case and hoped Louie might have some information that would break that case wide open.

They met in their usual place...in a narrow alley on the wrong side of the city. Sully distinctly remembered the scent of overripe trash rotting in the heat as he got out of his car and made his way toward the back of the alley. The moment he started walking toward the alley, a strange disquiet swept through him.

Louie was already there, pacing back and forth in characteristic nervous, jerky movements. Most snitches, in Sully's experience, were neurotic, paranoid worms, but they were useful to law enforcement.

As Sully made his way to the punk, he had a sudden feeling of suffocation, of the tall old brick buildings on either side of the alley pressing in on him. The stench of the garbage was overpowering and for a single moment, Sully had the impulse to turn and run. He had an odd premonition, a feeling of dread and impending doom.

He swallowed down the impulse to leave and continued until he reached Louie. "You got something for me?" he'd asked.

"You got something for me?" Louie scratched the side of his face, his eyes darting from building to building, as if he were afraid somebody might see him here with Sully.

"You know the way this works, Louie," Sully replied tersely, the feeling of something not right still whirling inside him. "You give me the information and I decide what it's worth."

"Maybe this time I want the bread first," Louie said with a touch of defiance. "And I'm not talking peanuts here. What I've got is worth big bucks to you, especially to you."

Sully never got the chance to find out what information Louie had. In the second of silence that followed Louie's statement, Sully heard a faint metallic click.

He froze.

The first bullet caught Louie in the forehead, and flung his body backward to crash into a pile of trashcans. The second shot caught Sully in the shoulder, spinning him around so that the third bullet could catch him dead center in the chest.

Sully's last thought before he lost consciousness was that maybe if he hadn't frozen when he heard that telltale sound, he might have been able to save Louie. He might have been able to save himself.

"Sully."

He jerked at the sound of his name, drawn from the past nightmare by Theresa's light touch on his arm. He opened his eyes and realized they were at the county jail.

Rubbing a hand down his face, he shoved his painful memories aside and focused on the particular pain at hand. Eric. If it was correct that some bad guy had taken him to hurt Theresa and Sully, then they were in big trouble, because Sully had long ago lost the ability to discern who were the good guys and who were the bad.

THERESA FOLLOWED Sully and Donny into the jail, where the sheriff awaited them. She knew that Roger Neiman knowing something, anything, about Eric's disappearance was a long shot, but it was the only shot they had. She'd never forgive herself if they didn't follow each and every lead, no matter how crazy each might initially appear.

She already knew Eric hadn't been hit by a car on his way to school, hadn't broken his leg or fallen unconscious. If that had been the case, the police scouring the area would have found him.

"I've got Neiman in a conference room for you all to talk to," the sheriff explained as he led them down a hall.

"Has he had any visitors in the last day or two?" Donny asked.

"His mother came the day after his conviction, but she hasn't been back. His brother's been here to see him every day 'cept today."

Theresa saw the look that passed between Sully and Donny, and she knew they both were thinking the same thoughts that swirled in her head. Maybe his brother hadn't been to see him today because he couldn't leave wherever he was holding Eric. Maybe they'd spent the past couple of days plotting and planning their revenge against the lady prosecutor who had relentlessly pursued justice.

She almost hoped Roger was behind Eric's disappearance. Then at least they'd have a place to begin to search, a reason for this happening.

Sometimes parents were left with no answers, no reasons and no final closure, a little voice whispered inside her head. The thought of never knowing what had happened to Eric, never getting to see his little face again, hold him in her arms, created a yawning chasm of blackness inside her heart, a blackness too profound to even consider.

Tears once again threatened, but she swallowed against them. Now was not the time to cry. She had to hang on to her hope, her belief that if something horrible had happened to Eric, she would know it deep in her heart. And right now, all her heart felt was worry and bewilderment, not aching, soul-withering grief.

It wasn't until the sheriff unlocked and opened the door to the conference room and Theresa saw Roger Neiman's narrow pale face, with its foxlike features, that the first stirring of anger coursed through her. Damn him. Damn him to hell if he was responsible for anything happening to Eric.

"These people got some questions for you, Neiman," the sheriff said.

Roger nodded and crossed his arms on the top of the table where he sat. A sly grin crossed his lips as his eyes locked with Theresa's. "Come to wish me happy holidays, Counselor?"

"Shut up, Neiman," Donny exclaimed, before Theresa could form any sort of a reply. Theresa was vaguely aware of Sully moving closer to her, as if in some way to show Roger Neiman she was not alone.

In some distant part of her mind, she found Sully's concern for her ironic. After all, it was he who had insisted she'd be better off alone, and there were days when she was grateful he had...and days when she hated him for abandoning her.

"We've got some questions to ask you, Neiman, and you'd better be straight with us," Donny said.

"Or what? You'll put me in jail?" Roger chortled, as if delighted by his own sense of humor.

Sully tensed, his hands balling into fists. Theresa placed a hand on his arm, needing him to control his anger, knowing they'd get nowhere if Sully lost his cool.

"Roger, my son is missing." Theresa stared at the young man, watching for any sign of guilt...a slight narrowing of his eyes, a little catch in his breathing pattern.

"Yeah...so? What's that got to do with me?" He looked first at Theresa, then at the other two men. His face paled and his eyes widened as he once again gazed at Theresa. "Hey, you don't think I had something to do with that? That's crazy!"

"Yeah, well, you aren't exactly studying for brain surgery in here," Donny replied. "Where's your brother today? Why didn't he come to see you?"

"I don't know.... He's out of town."

"Which is it? You don't know or he's out of town?" Donny snapped.

Theresa felt her tension swelling inside her. She saw defiance shining in Roger's eyes, and knew that if Donny pushed too hard, Roger would clam up. He had nothing to lose by keeping his mouth shut, and nothing to gain by talking.

She sat down in the chair next to him. "Roger, I did my job in prosecuting you. It was nothing personal, just my job. When you left the courtroom after your conviction, you yelled that I'd be sorry, that this would be a Christmas I'd never forget."

Roger flushed. "I was angry. I also told the judge I hoped his hair would all fall out. I said a lot of stupid things." He had eyes the color of caramels, surprisingly warm and beautiful. "Look, Mrs. Mathews, I'm no fool. I've got a good lawyer working on an appeal. Even if we lose an appeal, with good time served, I'll be out of jail in no time. Why would I risk that to do something stupid with your kid?"

A wave of utter helplessness swept through Theresa. Again she studied his features, stared into his eyes, looking for signs of guilt, of subterfuge. There was nothing there.

She believed him. Despite the fact that he had motive, and she knew he'd wanted to get to her, make her pay, she believed he'd had nothing to do with Eric's disappearance.

She stood and gestured toward the door. "Come on, let's go."

She and Donny started for the door, but paused

when Sully didn't follow. Theresa turned to see Sully slap his hands down on the table and lean across into Roger's face. "If we leave here and later I discover you knew something...anything...about Eric, I'll come back here and kill you."

Roger's eyes grew huge, and he scooted his chair back, as if to gain some distance from Sully's threat. "I swear, man. I don't know anything. I didn't even know she had a kid."

"Sully." Theresa spoke his name gently, knowing the raging emotion that filled him, the tight control he was fighting to maintain. He turned to face her, the gray of his eyes nearly black with torment. "Let's go home," she said softly.

He nodded and stalked out of the room. Theresa followed, a sense of dread crawling up her spine. With the strain of Eric being missing, how long would it be before Sully once again plunged into the self-destruction he'd only recently pulled himself out of? And what if this time he wouldn't find the strength or the reason to crawl out?

She couldn't go through it again. She couldn't stand to watch him drink himself to death, hate himself to death. She hadn't understood it the first time, and she had a feeling that if it happened again, she'd be the one who went mad.

The ride back to the house seemed interminably long, the car filled with a tense silence. Theresa looked at her watch. It was almost ten o'clock. After Eric's bedtime.

She leaned her head back, wondering when she

would tuck Eric in bed again, when would she sing the silly song he always demanded she sing to lull him into sleep?

With her eyes closed, she could conjure up a picture of him beneath his navy sheets, his hair softly tousled, the scent of his bath still clinging to his sweet skin.

"I'm still going to get some men to check up on Neiman's brother." Donny's voice dispelled the vision in her head. "What's his name?"

"Burt," she answered. "Burt Neiman."

"I think it's damned suspicious that he's been to see his brother in jail every day but today."

As they turned the corner of her block, Theresa stared out the window. As she caught sight of her house, her heart thundered. The Christmas lights that outlined the house had been turned off. Only the pale illumination from the front window glowed in the night.

"Who turned out the lights?" she muttered angrily as Donny parked the car amid the other patrol vehicles. The minute the car came to a halt, she flew out the door and raced to the side of the house, where the lights should have been plugged into the outside electrical socket. "Who unplugged the lights?" she screamed as she plugged them back in. The multicolored lights came on, a merry burst of color cascading across the brown lawn.

Donny and Sully stared at her, as if she'd lost her mind. And someplace in the back of her head, she knew she had, knew she was overreacting, and couldn't stop.

Kip stepped out on the porch, a sheepish expression on his face. "Uh...I turned them out.... I didn't think you'd want them on...." he explained.

"Dammit, these lights don't go off again until Eric is home." She glared at Kip, then turned to Donny. "You tell them. You tell all those men in there. Nobody touches these lights. Nobody shuts them off."

"Come on, Theresa. Let's go inside." Sully took her arm gently.

"It's Eric's job to turn them off. I turn them on in the evenings, and he unplugs them before he goes to bed. It's our deal." She looked at Sully, needing him to understand just how important Eric was to her.

"I know, and I'll make certain nobody touches those lights but Eric," Sully replied. "Now come on, let's go inside where it's warm."

Theresa bit back tears. "I don't think I'll ever be warm again," she said as Sully led her into the house.

Chapter Four

"Is she asleep?" Donny asked when Sully joined him in the kitchen sometime later.

"For the moment," Sully replied as he poured himself a cup of coffee, then sank down at the table. He raked a hand across his face, fighting exhaustion, battling despair.

"Everything that can be done is being done," Donny said, as if reading his mind. "I've got men checking out everything we can think of, all the people on the list Theresa made."

Sully nodded. He knew Donny and the team of officers would do whatever they could to find Eric. The problem was, so far they were banging their heads against dead ends. There were no clues, no discernible motives, no substantial leads to follow. Right now, they were merely spitting in the wind, hoping to get lucky. And Sully knew that with every minute that passed, the odds of finding Eric unharmed decreased.

"I guess the best we can hope for at this time is

that it is a kidnapping and whoever has Eric will make contact," he said.

"We've got wires on the phones. All incoming calls will be recorded and traced. I'm still hoping when we hear from the officers checking out Burt Neiman we'll have some answers."

Three days before Christmas, and he had no son, and wires on the phones. How had this happened? Why had this happened? Eric should be safe in bed, dreaming of sugarplums and candy canes, of Santa Claus and gaily wrapped presents.

Sully tightened his hand around the coffee mug. Dammit, he should be doing something, moving mountains, to find his son. But he didn't know which mountains to move.

"Can you think of anyone who might want to get at you?" Donny asked. "Somebody from that bar where you work?"

Sully thought for a moment, then shook his head. "Nobody I can think of. As a bouncer, the hardest work I do is escort drunks to waiting taxis and only occasionally break up a brawl. The patrons are usually too drunk to remember what I look like, let alone put something like this together."

For a few moments, the two men sat silent. Sully could hear the low murmur of the policemen in the living room, the sudden whoosh of heated air through pipes as the furnace came on. Beyond these noises, both intrusive and normal, was the yawning silence of Eric's absence. There was no silence as profound as that left behind by a child missing.

"Ever think of coming back to the department?" Donny asked after a few minutes of silence. "You know the chief would love to have you back on the roster."

"Nope, never think about it." It was a lie. Sully thought about going back to the department every morning after a night's work at the bar, just before he closed his eyes to sleep. He'd loved being a cop, and he'd been a damned good one, too. But those days were over. "I like what I'm doing now." Sully sipped his coffee and forced himself to relax. "I hear this is Chief Lewis's last year, that he's retiring."

Donny laughed. "You know the chief. Every year he says it's his last. We'll see what he decides when the time comes."

"You looking to fill his shoes?"

Donny blinked in surprise.

Sully laughed dryly. "Oh, come on, Donny. You're more ambitious than most. You play the political games well."

Donny grinned and shook his head. "I forgot how well you know me." He shrugged. "We'll see what happens when the time comes. Sure, I'd like to one day be chief." He studied Sully. "You would have been a logical candidate if..."

"If I hadn't believed my own press? The invincible Sullivan." Sully laughed without humor. "Or maybe I might have eventually made chief if I hadn't become a drunk?" He realized he was making Donny uncomfortable. "Sorry," he said as he pulled himself out of his chair and went to the window to peer outside.

"Sully, I didn't mean to reopen old wounds," Donny's voice was low and apologetic.

Sully turned around and stared at the man who'd been his partner for over two years. They'd been good together, worked well as two halves of a whole. Where Sully was sometimes impetuous, Donny was methodical. Sully's street smarts had been enhanced by Donny's book smarts.

"You didn't reopen them, they just haven't finished healing yet," Sully finally replied.

"Sully...I never really got a chance to tell you I'm—"

"Don't say it, Donny. You've got nothing to feel bad about. I should have known better than to meet Louie in that alley alone. I should have set the meet for another time. You don't owe me anything."

Donny seemed to visibly relax. A smile curved his lips. "But we did have some good times, didn't we? You still eat those god-awful burritos?"

Sully returned his smile. "You still like your pizza with little fish on top?"

Donny nodded. "Remember the case of Sullivan's stew?"

A burst of laughter slid from Sully, the laugh sounding rusty from little use. "How could I forget that one?" It had been the crazy kind of case that usually made for humorous television specials. A man had broken into a restaurant via a narrow skylight. He'd dropped to the floor, his foot landing directly in a stew pot. Unable to remove the pot, incapable of crawling back out the skylight with it stuck on his foot, he'd eventually had to call the police to rescue him.

Sully had made the arrest, and the newspapers had snapped a picture of him leading the man away in handcuffs...the foot firmly entrenched in the metal pot. Sullivan's Stew, the local headline had read the next morning.

For the next week, cans of stew had appeared in Sully's locker and at his desk as his fellow officers razzed him mercilessly.

The memory caused a bittersweet pang to sweep through Sully. That had been before somebody, one of his brother officers, betrayed him. Crazy thoughts, that was what Chief Lewis had told him when he voiced this particular suspicion. The resulting investigation had turned up nothing but the conclusion that whoever Louie was about to squeal on had shut him up permanently, and Sully had merely been at the wrong place at the wrong time.

In the weeks that Sully spent in the hospital recuperating from the bullet removed from his chest, his suspicions that the shooter had been after him had only increased, as had his instincts that somebody he'd trusted set him up. They were thoughts he hadn't voiced to anyone but the chief.

Now, with the passing of time, Sully no longer knew what to think. Maybe Chief Lewis had been right all along, and the instincts that had made Sully such a good cop had deserted him...along with his nerve.

He leaned his forehead against the cold windowpane, the past fluttering away as the present anxiety returned.

"We'll find him, Sully," Donny said. "If he can be found, I swear to you we'll find him."

Sully nodded and stared out the window, where gem-colored beams of light danced on the frozen ground. None of his past emotional baggage was important right now. What was important was that Eric be found, alive and well.

It had been a very long time since Sully said a prayer, but standing at the window, staring out into the dark of night, he prayed for Eric.

"ERIC!" Theresa sat straight up in bed, the dream so real, so tangible, that for a moment she was completely disoriented.

She stared around her. The hall light sent in a glow that pierced the darkness of the bedroom. Then she remembered...remembered it all...and she squeezed her eyes tightly closed, willing the tears away.

She refused to cry...to cry somehow felt like an abandonment of hope...and abandoning hope was like forsaking Eric.

Rolling over on her side, she stared at the digital clock next to the bed. Just after three o'clock. Dawn was still several hours away.

She sat up and rubbed her eyes. She had slept, although she hadn't intended to. She remembered

Sully sitting at the edge of her bed, encouraging her to rest for a little while. She didn't remember him leaving the room.

She got out of bed and raked a hand through her hair. She walked to the window and peered out into the darkness, her heart crying out in the night. *Eric, where are you? What's happening? Please, God, keep him safe...don't let him be afraid.* She turned away from the darkness, unable to look at it any longer, knowing that her son, her heart, was somewhere out there.

She left the bedroom and hesitated outside Eric's closed bedroom door. She placed her hand on the knob, fighting against the feeling that if she flung the door open fast enough, Eric would be there, tucked into bed, safe and sound. Taking a deep breath, she released her hold on the knob, knowing he hadn't miraculously been restored to her in the hours she slept.

In the living room, she found Kip Pearson stretched out on the sofa, his breathing deep and regular in the pattern of sleep.

The perfectly shaped pine tree stood in the corner, naked and sad without the ornaments to turn it into a splendid Christmas tree. They had been going to decorate it that night. Eric loved decorating the tree.

A light beneath the kitchen door beckoned her, and she welcomed the scent of coffee that drifted out, that spoke of companionship. She didn't want to be alone. She was afraid to be alone.

She entered the kitchen and found Sully sitting at

the table, a notebook in front of him. He looked up as she came in.

"Is that coffee fresh?" she asked.

He nodded. "And strong."

She poured herself a cup and sat down across from him. For a long moment, they merely looked at each other. Their past, both good and bad, didn't matter.

At this moment in time, they were simply two parents thrust into an unspeakable, an unthinkable, position. She reached across the table, and he met her hand halfway, enclosing hers in his.

She'd always loved Sully's hands. They were big and capable, with long, sensual fingers. She'd always believed his hands held some kind of magic. She'd always felt safe, secure, with her hand in his, but apparently the magic had fled with the demise of their marriage, for this time his hand surrounded hers with warmth, but couldn't banish the fear inside her heart.

"Where is everyone?" she asked.

"Donny went home. He'll be back in the morning. Some of the men left on other calls, others are still looking."

"I owe Kip an apology." She frowned, remembering those moments of rage when she'd seen that the outside lights had been turned off.

"Don't worry about it. He's a big boy. He knows you didn't mean anything personal. Did you manage to get some sleep?"

She nodded. "A little, but I had a horrible dream," she said. "Eric was lost in a dark fog. He was calling for me, but I couldn't find him.'' Sully's hand tightened around hers. ''The fog was so thick. He kept calling, 'Mommy...Mommy, help me,' and just when I'd think I was closer...within touching distance...his voice would move further away....'' She broke off.

She couldn't lose hope. Hope was all she had, and somehow, in losing hope, she felt she'd lose a piece of Eric. ''He's alive,'' she said fervently. ''I know all about the statistics, I know with each moment that passes the odds are against it, but I know he's still alive. I feel him here.'' She placed a hand over her heart.

Sully's gray eyes darkened. ''I'd move heaven and hell to find him, but I don't know where to begin.'' He released her hand and jerked himself up out of his chair. ''Dammit, this is what I did for years.... I was a cop, and yet I can't do a damn thing to find my son.''

His voice was filled with a helplessness that tore at Theresa's heart. She stood and went to him, put her arms around him. He hugged her tight, burrowing his face in her hair. They clung together like two weary sailors in a storm-tossed sea.

Despite the fact that it had been almost a year since she was held in his arms for any length of time, immediately her body conformed to the familiarity of his. There was comfort in his very solidness, in the scent of him and the feel of his large hands against her back.

She suddenly remembered how his hands had

rubbed her back and her legs when she was in labor with Eric. Her pains had focused in those areas, and Sully had patiently, lovingly massaged her for hours.

At that time, she'd felt as if she were as big as a whale, her hair had been limp and sweaty from the hours of hard labor, and yet Sully's eyes, when he looked at her, had been filled with such love, such utter devotion, when she finally gave birth to Eric.

Oh, God, how she wished she could feel indifferent toward him after all this time. How she wished her heart didn't still ache with the wonder and despair of loving him. Once loving him, she corrected herself as she stepped out of his embrace.

She refused to get caught up in the misery of loving Sully now. Something had happened to him when that bullet hit him. Not only had it broken ribs and torn muscle, it had also destroyed a piece of him that allowed him to love.

"So what happens now?" she asked as she sat down at the table again.

He shrugged. "First thing in the morning, we'll start circulating Eric's picture, hanging posters. The police will do more interviews. Somebody had to see something, and all they need to do is connect with that person." He, too, sat down at the table, his gaze not quite meeting hers. "You know that with every hour that passes the odds are against us that Eric's just going to call and say he's lost."

Theresa nodded, trying to get beyond her need to scream, clutching to her a numbing shield that she knew would allow her to function most efficiently.

"So, if he hasn't gotten lost, and he's not lying unconscious in a ditch somewhere, that leaves only one option left—he's been abducted." Her hand trembled slightly as she reached for her coffee cup. "And that leaves another question...was he taken for a specific reason by somebody we know, or is it a stranger abduction?"

Sully looked at her in surprise. "You should have been a cop."

She forced a thin smile. "I was once married to one."

Her words fell heavily and immediately created an uncomfortable silence. Theresa sought words to say, words that would create a comfort zone for them both. She needed to feel a connection to Sully, but knew that in the past year their connection had been pared down to a single thing...their shared parenting of Eric.

She wanted conversation to pass the time, fill the emptiness, but it saddened her to realize she didn't know what to talk to Sully about...what would be considered off-limits and what topic would be all right. How much they'd lost...how far they'd drifted from one another.

She watched as Sully left the table and leaned against the counter near the refrigerator. He looked around the kitchen. "You've got a nice place here, Theresa. Warm and inviting. It feels like a home." He moved to the back door and peered out, then turned to face her. "Eric tells me you're planning on having a patio put in next summer."

"Yeah, Eric keeps insisting we need a patio with a cool brick barbecue pit so he can take over the cooking duties in the summer."

"Eric's happy here. He likes the neighborhood, likes this house. He talks about it all the time when he visits me. He's happy here," he repeated. "You made a good choice moving here."

Theresa stared down at the tabletop. Had she made a good choice? Or had she moved him to a place of danger? If she'd chosen anyplace else on earth to live, would Eric be sleeping safe in his bed at the moment? Had she remained in the midtown condo, would any of this have happened?

"Don't." The single word eased out of Sully. She looked at him in surprise. "Don't blame yourself, Theresa. This has nothing to do with your decision to live here. It has nothing to do with us or our divorce. We can't expend valuable energy blaming ourselves."

Theresa got up once again and walked to the window. "Night is the hardest, isn't it?" she said softly.

"Night is always the hardest," he agreed. "Daylight always brings with it endless possibilities. The night seems to hold nothing but emptiness."

She turned and looked at him curiously. "Is that why you work the night shift at that bar? So you don't have to face the empty nights?"

He smiled without humor. "I work at the bar to pay my bills."

She knew he was shutting her out, keeping her from knowing the workings of his heart. He'd become good at that after the shooting, closing himself into isolation. "But...why a bar, Sully? Especially since..."

"Since I'm a drunk?"

She flushed. "I didn't say that."

"You didn't have to. It's common knowledge." He sighed and raked a hand through his dark hair. "I took the job in the bar to prove that I could work in a place that served booze, and not give in to the need to drink."

Theresa felt a ghost of a smile lift the corners of her mouth. "You always were a perverse cuss, Sullivan Mathews." She turned back to stare, unseeing, out the window, wondering if this night would ever pass.

ERIC AWOKE from a bad dream. In his nightmare, somebody had put a stinky old rag over his nose and mouth and carried him to a dark and scary place.

As sleep ebbed, he cautiously opened his eyes and searched for his familiar posters, his hamster, Petey...the night-light that chased away goblins and creepy things in the dark.

A single high window was on the wall above his head, a window covered with thick boards. Dawn light seeped in between the slats of wood, making tiny patterns on the concrete walls.

No posters. No Petey. It hadn't been a dream. It was real. Oh, God, it was real.

His stomach rolled, and shiver bumps popped up on his skin. He felt just like he had a month before, when he got the flu. His mom had given him peppermint medicine and soda over chips of ice. But he knew with dreadful certainty that his mom wasn't anywhere around. There was no way she would allow him to sleep in a room so cold, on a bed that smelled yucky and had no sheets.

His gaze darted around the room. All cement walls and a concrete floor. A set of wooden stairs led up to a slanted door. He knew it was a cellar. His friend Bobby had a cellar, and they'd often play down there, even though Bobby's mom got mad at them.

His sense of panic receded as another, more pressing problem appeared. He had to go to the bathroom...bad. He had to go so bad he felt like he was going to explode. But there was no way he was going to wet his pants. He wasn't a baby anymore. Still, he had to find someplace to go...immediately.

Once again he gazed around, this time more desperately. The corners of the room were dark shadows holding unknown terrors. He eyed the stairs and the door at the top.

Cautiously he tiptoed up the seven stairs and tried to turn the knob of the door. Locked. He fought the impulse to bang on the door, scream out the terror that choked his throat. He was afraid to scream, afraid to let anyone know he was awake. He was afraid of who...or what...might open the door.

He walked back down the stairs and sat on the bottom step, his bladder aching with fullness. What was he supposed to do? He couldn't remember the last time he'd wet his pants, although he'd had an accident in his bed last year, when he was sick and the doctor gave him medicine that made him sleepy. His mom had told him it wasn't his fault.

He half turned on the stair where he sat and peered beneath the stairway. That was when he saw it. He knew immediately what it was, because Jimmy Baker and his parents had taken Eric on a camping trip and they had used one for a weekend. A portable toilet.

It wasn't until he'd relieved himself that his fear returned. Where was he? Who had put him down here, and why? He stood on the bed and tried to peer out between the boards on the window, but they were too close together to allow him to see out.

Still, he could vaguely smell the odor of the country and hear insects clicking and chirping. What he couldn't hear was the noise of any traffic or the sounds he could always hear from his bedroom window.

Surely his mom and dad would find him anytime now. If it was morning, then he'd been gone a whole day. They probably had a million cops looking for him. His dad had been a cop. He'd find Eric.

Eric froze when he heard footsteps over his head. Somebody was coming. "Mom?" he whispered hopefully, the sick feeling returning to his stomach. "Mommy?" His voice sounded funny as it bounced off the concrete walls. "Hey, I'm down here! Help me!" His terror released itself in his screams. And he might have gone on screaming forever, if the door at the top of the stairs hadn't opened, the creaking noise causing him to fall silent. He stared up with a mixture of wild anticipation and horrifying dread.

A set of legs appeared in his vision, then a body, and finally a head, covered with a black ski mask. Eric pressed himself against the corner, shoving a fist into his mouth to keep himself from crying.

A man...Eric knew it was a man, but the ski mask hid everything except the glittering eyes. The eyes were scary. They glittered like a cat's eyes in the dark.

"Who...who are you? What do you want?" he asked. His voice sounded little and small. "Why are you doing this to me?" To his horror, tears burned at his eyes. He didn't want to cry. He didn't want to show that he was afraid. "My mom and dad are gonna kill you if you don't take me back," he added, with a burst of bravery that lasted only a moment.

The man never said a word, and for the first time, Eric noticed that he carried a grocery sack. He set the sack down on the floor, then turned and went back up the stairs.

"Hey...hey, wait!" Eric cried, terrified of the man, yet more terrified of being left all alone. "Wait... Tell me what's happening? Why are you doing this?"

The door banged shut, and Eric heard the click of the lock being turned. He captured a sob in the palm of his hand. He couldn't cry. Joe Montana would never cry. When the pressure was on, Joe got cool. Joe stayed calm and in control.

Eric took several deep breaths, eyeing the brown

paper sack on the floor. What was in it? What if it was something horrible? What if it was filled with snakes? He didn't like snakes. He whimpered, able to imagine eel-like creatures slithering over the top, spilling out onto the floor, wrapping around him and squeezing him to death.

He closed his eyes to dispel the image and stared at the sack once again. It didn't crackle or move as if it contained anything alive.

He got up and walked over, peering down into the open mouth of the sack. Food. A package of sweet rolls, four store-bought sandwiches, a bag of barbecue chips, a package of cookies and a six-pack of orange soda. At the very bottom of the sack was a dozen comic books. They weren't his favorites, but they were ones he hadn't read.

What did it mean? What did it all mean?

Carefully Eric lined the food up on the bed, staring at it in bewilderment. His stomach growled, and he realized he was hungry. He tore open the cinnamon-roll package and ate one while he thought.

If the man had brought him here to kill him, then why bring him food? He suddenly remembered Hansel and Gretel, fattened up by the wicked witch so they would make a good meal when pushed into the stove.

But that was just a dumb old fairy tale and had nothing to do with real life. He finished the sweet roll, licking the cinnamon residue off his fingers. He wanted another one, but was afraid to eat too much.

After all, it might take a while for the police to

figure out where he was. What if he was down here for a long time? How long would this food have to last? Would the man come back? Again panic crawled up in the back of his throat, refusing to be swallowed and banished.

He placed the food back in the bag, then stretched out on the bed, fighting back tears. *Don't cry,* he told himself. *Joe doesn't cry.*

He closed his eyes, envisioning a football field and a cast of players. "And there's the snap. Joe rolls out of the pocket.... He evades one tackle...then another.... He pumps and throws. A perfect pass. He's great under pressure...great."

Eric curled himself into a ball on the mattress, a smile curving his lips as his panic slowly ebbed. He'd be okay. Like Joe, Eric knew he'd be great under pressure.

His smile slowly faded. He just hoped his mom and dad and the police hurried and found him. After all, even the great Joe Montana occasionally got sacked.

Chapter Five

December 23

Dawn didn't creep softly in, but rather arrived with an explosion of activity and the first appearance of the press, who knew the story of a child missing two days before Christmas had all the ingredients to evoke reader pathos, sell newspapers and raise television shares. The press members gathered on the sidewalk outside, like vultures waiting for a feast.

Kip Pearson had left the house sometime in the hours before dawn, and Sully and Theresa had taken short catnaps, taking turns on the sofa and in the overstuffed chair nearby.

In those long, torturous predawn hours, policemen drifted in, checking with the officer in charge, who had usurped the kitchen table as his base of command.

Theresa sat in the overstuffed chair in the living room, watching Sully sleep, as the first kiss of dawn slowly lit the room. He slept soundly, his breathing rhythm unbroken in the depth of sleep. She'd always been amazed by how easily Sully surrendered to sleep. No matter what emotional turmoil he felt, no matter what kind of stress he was under, he only had to get comfortable and close his eyes, and sleep came to him. She'd always envied him that.

She stretched, her gaze once again going to the window. The long, frightening night was over...but a new, equally frightening day had taken its place.

She was exhausted, but she knew it was an exhaustion no amount of sleep would cure. It was a spirit-tiredness that could only heal when her baby was back safe in her arms.

She was beginning to wonder if and when this nightmare would ever be over. Not if...when. *If* held too many possibilities for grief.

Getting up and walking over to the tree, she thought of the last Christmas the three of them had shared together. Although she desperately hoped Eric wasn't aware of it, the tension between Sully and Theresa had been horrible. But she'd known Eric felt the unhappiness in the air. By the New Year, Sully and Theresa had separated, and two months later their divorce had been finalized.

It didn't seem fair that for two years in a row Eric would be cheated out of a normal, happy Christmas. First by the failings of his parents, and now by this.

She touched the bough of the tree and drew in deeply of the sweet pine scent. She needed to decorate it. Hang the tinsel and the ornaments, the garland and the lights. Eric would expect a fully bedecked Christmas tree when he got home.

"Theresa?"

She turned at the sound of Sully's voice. Stretched out on the sofa, his eyes the color of a cloud-filled day, he looked tired, but so achingly handsome that her heart momentarily skipped a beat.

"You okay?" he asked.

He sat up and patted the sofa next to him. She walked over and sank into the cushions, which still retained the heat from his body. He placed an arm around her shoulders, and she leaned into him.

"I was just thinking that I need to decorate the tree. Eric will be unhappy when he gets home and it's not done. We always do it the evening of the twenty-second. I'll do it today. That way he won't be upset when he gets home."

"Theresa..." His arm tightened around her shoulders.

"Don't say it, Sully. I can't bear to hear that he might not be here for Christmas." She pulled away from him and faced him, seeing the cynicism that darkened his eyes. "I have to believe he'll be back home. I have to keep the faith. That's what Christmas is all about, isn't it?" She closed her eyes for a moment. "I have to believe this house, our love for Eric, is like the North Star, and it will eventually lead Eric back to us. To think otherwise is absolutely unacceptable."

"I'll help you decorate the tree."

Sully's offer, spoken softly, touched her. She knew he approached this from a different place. As a cop, he'd seen too much, experienced too much, to be optimistic. She knew he'd lost his faith, his hope, a long time ago. But she wasn't about to let him give up on Eric.

Any further talk was interrupted as a wave of policemen entered the house, one of them holding a stack of posters. Kip Pearson was among them.

Sully stood up from the sofa and greeted the middle-aged man. "I thought you were working that burglary case."

"I was. But I requested to be put on this case." Kip smiled at Sully, then at Theresa. "We're going to find your boy, and when we do, I'll treat you to a steak dinner at Harvey's."

Sully clapped Kip on the back, obviously touched by Kip's presence. "Thanks, man, I appreciate your support. Besides, in any case, it's your turn to pay for dinner. I paid last time."

Kip grinned. "No problem," he replied, then followed the other officers into the kitchen.

"I didn't realize you and Kip had become such friends," Theresa said when she and Sully were once again alone in the living room.

Sully swept a hand through his sleep-tousled hair. "You remember when I was in the hospital, Kip came to see me almost every day. After I quit the department, he's one of the few who has kept in touch with me." He hesitated a moment, then continued. "Kip was shot five years ago in the line of duty. He understood some of what I was going through."

Theresa fought against an edge of resentment at

his words, the implication that Kip had been there for him when she had not.

Certainly, Theresa had tried to understand both the physical and the emotional pain Sully experienced. But it was difficult to understand when the person suffering had closed himself off so effectively. Apparently he'd invited Kip into some of the dark spaces in his soul...spaces he hadn't allowed Theresa to enter.

The ringing of the phone sliced through Theresa's lingering resentment, effectively banishing all other thoughts from her mind.

Officer Jeffrey Ryder, the man in charge during Donny's absence, poked his head into the living room and motioned her toward the kitchen phone, where the tracing and recording equipment had been set up.

Ryder turned on the equipment and gestured for Theresa to answer the phone. She reached for Sully's hand, and for the receiver with the other hand. "Hello?" Her voice boomed from the speaker on the counter, allowing everyone in the room to hear.

"I know where your boy is." The female voice filled the kitchen. Sully's hand tightened around Theresa's.

"Who...who is this?"

"It doesn't matter who I am." Slightly hoarse, the voice sounded like an old woman's. "What matters is what you must do to get your boy back."

"Please...please don't hurt him." Theresa choked out the words, fighting the tears that burned at her eyes. "We'll do whatever you want, but please don't hurt Eric."

"I won't hurt the little lad, but I can't promise what those that have him might do."

"Just tell me what you want." Theresa was vaguely aware of Officer Ryder writing something down on a pad. He tore the paper off and handed it to another policeman, who quickly left the kitchen.

"This is what you must do...find a plump black cat and feed it fish for the next seven days."

"Pardon me?" Theresa wondered if perhaps she'd heard wrong.

"After the seven days are up, clip the whiskers and bury them in the backyard."

"Who is this?" she cried.

Sully released Theresa's hand and depressed the button, hanging up the call. "Dammit!" he thundered. "Word must be out, if the cranks have begun."

"Why would somebody do that?" Theresa asked, staring at the phone in horror. "Who would be so cruel?"

"A car is on the way to the house where the call generated," Officer Ryder said. "We'll probably find a lonely old lady who's gone off her medication." He walked over to the window and peered outside. "The press is all over the yard. Maybe an official statement will help." He looked at Theresa, then Sully. "Either one of you want to talk to them? Who knows, it might help. The more people we've got looking for Eric, the better our chances of finding him."

Theresa looked at Sully. The thought of going in front of cameras, telling the world about Eric's disappearance, suddenly made it painfully real.

"We'll talk to them," Sully said after a moment's hesitation. "We'll do it together." Once again he reached for her hand, and she grasped it tightly, as if it were a lifeline thrown to save her from drowning.

Minutes later, Theresa and Sully left the house and walked toward the bevy of reporters, who'd set up on the sidewalk, where they couldn't be thrown off private property.

Sully greeted several of the reporters by name, and Theresa knew many of them had written stories about Sully in the past...stories of his shining courage, his undaunted quest for justice. Mercifully, none had written of his fall from grace.

Both Sully and Theresa carried a handful of the posters that had been printed up at some point overnight. The brief interview passed in a fog for Theresa, who couldn't seem to stop clutching the posters that depicted the sweet, smiling face of her son.

It was a good picture, showing the shine of Eric's dark hair, not a strand out of place. His blue eyes radiated intelligence, good humor, and the self-confidence of a child who knew he was loved. The only things real for Theresa about this impromptu press conference were Eric's face and Sully's arm around her shoulders.

Sully handled the reporters adroitly, explaining the facts of Eric's disappearance and dancing around more personal, painful questions. He kept it short, pausing only long enough to hand out posters, then guided Theresa back to the house as more questions barraged them.

"How did they hear about this?" Theresa asked once they were back inside the house. "That crank caller...and all the reporters...how do they know about Eric?"

"Police scanners. The press follows the action they hear coming across the scanners, and the crank calls are usually shut-ins who also monitor police bands," Officer Ryder explained.

A scuffle at the front door drew their attention. "Let me by," a deep voice demanded.

Theresa immediately recognized the voice. "It's Robert...a friend of mine."

Officer Ryder nodded to the uniform at the front door. Robert burst into the house, his gaze immediately finding Theresa. "Terri...I just heard. I came as fast as I could." He embraced her in a hug, engulfing her with the scent of his expensive cologne. "Has there been any news? What can I do to help?" He stepped back from her, framing her face with his hands. "Are you all right? You doing okay?"

She nodded and stepped away from him, finding it vaguely uncomfortable for him to be touching her, hugging her, while Sully stood nearby.

Robert Cassino was the vice president of the bank where Theresa had her account. They had met soon after Theresa moved here, and in the past two months they'd had dinner together several times.

Robert, with his pretty features and suave demeanor, had become a friend in the past couple of months, but Theresa knew he hoped the relationship would evolve into something more.

"Sully...this is Robert Cassino, a friend of mine. Robert, my ex-husband, Sully."

The two men shook hands, then separated like two boxers going to their respective corners. "Now, what can I do to help?" Robert turned to Theresa, his blue eyes shining with earnest intent.

Theresa shrugged helplessly. "Everything that can be done is being done by the police."

"You can put up posters." Sully grabbed a handful of the blown-up pictures of Eric and thrust them into Robert's hands. "We need these hung all over the city, and the police don't have the manpower to get it done."

Robert looked down at the posters, then at Sully, finally back to Theresa. "Maybe you'd rather I just stay here—you know, be supportive for you."

"The posters need to be distributed," Theresa replied gently. She didn't want to hurt his feelings, but she couldn't deal with him now.

"I think I'll head back to my apartment," Sully said. "I need to shower and change clothes."

Robert smiled in what appeared to Theresa to be relief. "And I'll just get on my way to hang these posters."

Theresa walked with Robert to the door. "Thank you," she said.

"I'll be back later...as soon as I get these hung. I've already called the bank and told them I won't be in today." He leaned over and gave her a kiss on the cheek. "It's going to be all right."

When Robert had gone, Theresa turned back to Sully. "Robert works where I bank. We've had dinner a couple of times."

"You don't owe me any explanations," he replied tersely. "Besides, Eric has mentioned him to me. Eric doesn't like him."

"Eric still thinks we're going to get back together."

Sully held her gaze for a long moment, then raked a hand through his hair. "Yeah, well, he still believes in Santa Claus, too."

Theresa didn't know how it was possible that Sully still had the capacity to hurt her, but his words did just that. She held no illusions about her relationship with Sully. He'd left her, insisted he no longer desired a life with her. Even something as traumatic as Eric's disappearance couldn't change that fact. So why did he still have the power to hurt her?

"I'd better head home. I need to check on my answering machine. Maybe some message about Eric has been left there."

"Can't you call and get any messages from here?" She didn't want him to leave, wanted him to stay here with her. Although she knew this was no time to entertain thoughts of Sully and their past relationship, no time for old hurts or new wounds, his mere presence somehow comforted her.

He shook his head. "I need to go home. I've got some things to take care of that can't be taken care of from here."

She took a step back, mentally distanced herself from him. She mustn't depend on Sully. He was only in her life at the moment because of Eric. She had to focus on Eric. He was what was important now. "If there's any news at all, please call."

He nodded and left.

The moment he was gone, the house seemed to expand around her, growing large and cavernous, and achingly silent without Eric's laughter. She walked over to the sofa and sat, feeling like an outsider in her own house. Her home had been invaded by strangers in blue uniforms. They were in the kitchen, in Eric's room, drifting in and out of the front door.

Vaguely she wondered why Rose and Vincent hadn't been by to see what all the commotion was about. Normally, Rose seemed to know the neighborhood gossip practically before it happened. Why hadn't she heard from them?

The phone rang, and she jumped up and raced to the kitchen, where Officer Ryder stood ready. For the second time that morning, Theresa picked up the receiver, hoping for answers, praying for explanations.

"This is Mary Kelly with Channel Nine news," a pleasant voice said.

"We've already given a statement," Theresa replied, her breath whooshing out of her in disappointment. "Please...I don't want to tie up this line."

"Just a few questions, Mrs. Mathews..."

Theresa hung up and looked at the police officer in despair. The phone rang again.

"It looks like it's going to be a long day," Officer Ryder said sympathetically.

"Yes..." Theresa closed her eyes, fighting to remain strong.

SULLY UNLOCKED his apartment door and immediately heard the whimpers of the puppy. The whimpers turned into yips of delight when he walked into the living room and the puppy caught sight of him. Seeing that his answering machine had no calls, he walked over to the pen.

"Hey, little buddy." Sully opened the door of the pet enclosure and the pooch barreled out, slathering Sully's face with his tongue.

Sully burrowed his head in the dog's soft fur, seeking some solace from the relentless ache in his heart. Eric...where are you, my son? What's happened to you? How did a nine-year-old little boy disappear without a witness, without a clue?

Sully had once believed himself to be a strong man, but the past eighteen months of his life had proved otherwise to him.

How long could he suffer Eric's disappearance and not be lured back into the bottom of a bottle? He knew the seduction of booze, the promise of oblivion, the release of pain, that lay in the bottom of every bottle. How long before he plunged back into the pit of self-destruction and depression? *You're a loser...just like your old man,* a little voice whispered.

He shook his head, refusing to entertain black thoughts any longer. Putting the dog back in the pen, he added fresh food and water, then stumbled toward the bathroom and a good, hot shower.

As he stood beneath the hot spray, he thought of Robert Cassino. His instant gut reaction had been an intense dislike of the well-dressed, handsome man. It had begun with the handshake, when Robert squeezed his hand with a subtle show of macho challenge.

Or had it begun before that...the moment Robert framed Theresa's face with his hands? His fingers had moved lightly, covetously, against Theresa's skin.

Terri. He'd called Theresa Terri, as if it were an intimate pet name. Sully ducked his head beneath the needles of water. What did he care who touched Theresa? He didn't have a right to care.

Still, he could easily remember the soft texture of her skin beneath his fingertips, the spill of her thick hair across his chest as they'd made love.

He closed his eyes. It had been an eternity since he allowed himself to remember the physical aspects of their marriage. They'd enjoyed an intense, passionate physical relationship up until the night of the shooting.

Theresa, who always maintained such tight control

over herself in every other area, had lost control when making love. And her ultimate surrender while in his arms had always made the entire experience unforgettable for Sully.

Unforgettable. And yet he had to forget. He had to forget the taste of her lips, the way she'd moaned so deep in her throat when he caressed her, how she'd eagerly arched to meet his thrusts. He must forget the sweet way she'd cried out his name at the moment of release.

Muttering a curse beneath his breath, he turned the faucet to make the spray cold. He had to forget he'd ever loved Theresa. He'd made his bed, chosen his path, and it was one he intended to walk alone.

He shut off the water, shivering as he grabbed a towel and dried off. He consciously shoved away thoughts of his ex-wife and instead focused on Eric as he dressed.

Was it possible Eric had run away in some misguided effort to reunite Sully and Theresa? Eric had certainly made it clear that he wanted his parents back together again. Sully mulled that over as he pulled a sweater over his head.

No. That just wasn't possible. Eric wouldn't intentionally cause his parents such worry. He was a good kid, with a caring heart. Besides, no kid his age would be able to stay away from home for such an extended period of time. At the age of nine, an hour could be an eternity.

One thing gave Sully a small measure of comfort. Eric was smart. If there was a way for him to make his way home, he would. If he was being held against his will, his captors just might underestimate him. Unless it was already too late...unless he was already...

Sully drew in a deep breath, refusing to allow his thoughts to go farther. He had to believe it wasn't too late, had to believe that somehow Eric would be returned safe and sound to them.

Eric was not only the child of Sully's heart...he was the hope of the future, the promise of dreams fulfilled. Eric was the glue that held Sully together.

He started out of his bedroom, then paused and instead went to the top dresser drawer. There, amid rolled-up socks and cotton briefs, was a .38 automatic.

Sully had turned in his police-issue weapon when he quit the department, but he'd kept his personal piece, although it hadn't been out of this drawer, except for monthly cleanings, for years.

He picked it up, the balance and weight feeling right in his hand. Crazy. What made him think he'd need a gun? There were dozens of cops on the case...real cops. He had no business even considering taking the gun with him. He should leave the gunplay to the professionals. Still, when he left the room a moment later, the gun was tucked into his waistband.

Before leaving to return to Theresa's, he took a moment and forwarded his calls to her phone, unwilling to take the risk of missing a call from a possible kidnapper.

He pulled his coat on, then stared at the dog, who sat on furry haunches, eyeing him soulfully. "Theresa is going to kill me," he muttered as he opened the pen and slipped a leash on to the dog collar.

He couldn't leave the dog here. He had no idea when he would return. Besides, the dog was for Eric, and should be waiting at the house for Eric's return. Yes, Theresa was probably going to kill him, but he didn't care.

"Come on, Montana. Let's go bye-bye." The dog barked cheerfully at his name and tugged Sully toward the front door.

Chapter Six

The moment Sully pulled in front of Theresa's, he knew something had happened. An intensity swirled in the air as police scurried in and out of the house. As Sully led Montana toward the front door, Sully instantly felt the vibration of energy in his gut.

"Sully, thank God you're back," Theresa said as he walked in the door. She frowned at the dog. "What's that?"

"It's a dog. It's Eric's Christmas present. Meet Montana." Sully saw the tightening of her jaw. "I know...I know, I should have asked you, but I didn't. And I couldn't leave him alone in my apartment. He belongs here...waiting for Eric."

The tightening of her jaw eased. "Oh, Sully," she said softly. "We'll put him in Eric's room for now." She took the leash from him and led the dog into Eric's bedroom, then closed the door. When she turned back to Sully, her eyes were shining with suppressed excitement. "They think they found Eric's book bag."

"Where?" Sully asked, his stomach muscles clenched. Finally...finally, a break.

"Someplace over by the school. A couple of officers left a little while ago to pick it up and question the man who has it."

Dammit. The first real break in the case, and Sully hadn't been here. He'd have wanted to go with the officers, talk to whoever it was who had the bag. "How long ago did they leave?"

"Just a few minutes ago."

He realized that while he was gone, Theresa had apparently showered and changed her clothes. Her dark hair was still damp, and the faint scent of fresh shampoo emanated from it. She wore a pair of black sweatpants and a peach-and-black sweatshirt, the peach tones bringing out the matching hues of her skin.

"Where's Ryder?" Sully asked, trying to stay focused on the matter at hand.

"In the kitchen. They assigned a female officer to answer the phone. It's been ringing off the wall since you left...mostly reporters and cranks." As if to punctuate her sentence, the phone rang.

"Come on, let's check it out," Sully said as he took her arm and led her into the kitchen.

"Please...don't call here again. We're trying to keep this line open," a female cop said into the receiver. She slammed down the phone. "Damn reporters," she muttered.

"What's this about a book bag?" Sully asked Jeffrey Ryder, who sat at the table, a cup of coffee and a donut before him.

Jeffrey shrugged and washed down a bite of donut with a swig of coffee. "All we know is some old guy called and said he'd found a book bag on the sidewalk yesterday afternoon. Knowing the forecast was for possible snow, he brought the bag into his house. When he heard about Eric this morning, he thought maybe he should call the police." He gestured to the box of donuts on the counter. "Help yourself."

Sully shook his head. Even though logically he knew the man needed to eat, it seemed obscene that he was sitting at the table enjoying a long john while Eric was God knew where.

"I called the phone company and had them forward any calls that might come into my apartment here," Sully said.

"Good idea," Jeffrey replied. "If this is a kidnapping, we can't guess who the perp might contact for a ransom."

"If there is a ransom demand," Sully said, then instantly regretted it.

"What do you mean, if?" Theresa asked. She searched his features intently. "If somebody kidnapped Eric, then surely they'd demand a ransom before returning him."

"Unless this is strictly a revenge plot and they don't intend to return him." Sully hated himself for saying the words aloud, for being the cause of Theresa's face paling and her eyes blackening with despair. But she had to know.

She had to know what the possibilities were. Eric had been gone over twenty-four hours, and Theresa had to begin to prepare herself for whatever might come. Just as Sully recognized he had to begin to prepare himself. But how do you prepare for something like that? he wondered.

As they waited for the men to return from checking out the book bag, Donny returned to the scene. "I couldn't sleep," he admitted sheepishly. "I have a feeling I won't be able to until we find Eric."

Emotion clogged Sully's throat. He nodded to Donny, unable to speak, grateful nothing was expected from him. He'd forgotten the brotherhood that existed among the ranks of the officers, a brotherhood he'd turned his back on because of his own paranoid suspicions.

At this moment in time, Sully knew Donny and Kip, and all the other men working the case, viewed him not only as a grieving parent, but also as one of their own. It made his suspicions concerning his shooting seem small and petty and without warrant.

The back door opened, and Kip and another officer walked in. "We got it!" Kip exclaimed, and held up a brown paper bag that apparently contained the piece of evidence. Taking the bag by the bottom, he dumped the contents on the table.

A small cry escaped Theresa, confirming that the blue backpack was, indeed, Eric's. She sat down at the table, her gaze not wavering from the bag.

"What did you find out?" Sully asked. Then, realizing he was stepping on Donny's toes, he clamped his mouth firmly shut.

"The old man's story seems to be on the up-and-up," Kip explained. "He saw the backpack about noon yesterday, realized it might snow and took it in the house, figuring he'd take it to the school after the holidays and turn it in to the lost and found. He didn't think any more about it until he heard a news report this morning about a kid missing, then he figured he'd better let somebody know he had it."

"Have you checked the bag?" Donny asked.

Kip shook his head. Donny patted his pockets, then frowned. "Anyone got a pair of gloves?"

Kip handed him a pair of latex gloves and, after pulling them on, Donny pulled the bag toward him.

As Donny pulled the zipper to open the bag, it seemed as if everyone in the room held their breath. Sully's gaze sought Theresa's, and in her eyes he saw the same thoughts going through his head.

Would there be a ransom note tucked inside? Was the bag covered with the fingerprints of the person who had Eric...or someone who knew what had happened to him?

Donny pulled from the bag a math book, a thin spiral notepad, several pencils and a squashed, half-eaten Twinkie. An unintelligible sound escaped from Theresa at the sight of the flattened Twinkie.

"I've told that kid a million times not to put food in his book bag," she said, her eyes overbright with emotion.

"That's it," Donny said, then opened one of the three pockets on the side of the bag. The first two were empty. The third yielded a neatly folded piece of paper.

Sully heard Theresa's audible intake of breath, felt the palpable tension that screamed silently in the air as Donny carefully unfolded the paper.

Donny scanned the contents quickly, then slammed a fist down on the table and tossed the note into the center for them all to see.

It was a love note, or as close to a love note as a fourth-grade boy could write.

Dear Susan. I like you. Do you like me. I think your frekles are cute.

Love, Eric.

P.S. if you tell anyone about this...I'll sock you.

Sully stared at the words, written in Eric's boyish scrawl, and his heart constricted painfully. Eric had probably intended to give Susan this note at school yesterday. But Eric hadn't made it to school.

He looked up to where Theresa had sat only moments before. The chair was empty. She wasn't in the kitchen, nor was she in the living room.

Sully walked down the hallway, stopping in front of Eric's closed bedroom door. Vaguely, through the barrier of the door, he could hear the sound of soft sobbing.

He leaned his forehead against the hard wood of the door, unsure whether to go into the room or not.

Theresa had always been very private with her emotions.

He'd stood next to her when her mother died, and she hadn't shed a tear in his presence. It had only been later, when she went to take a shower, that he heard the sounds of her grief over the spray of the water. When she came out of the bathroom, she'd been strong, in control, the only evidence of her crying the slightly red, swollen condition of her eyes.

He'd always admired her strength, and that was why, when he lost all of his, fell apart at the seams, he'd refused to hang around for her to see the wreck he'd become.

He opened the door about an inch, just enough to peek in and make sure she was all right. She was lying on Eric's narrow twin bed, her arms wrapped around Montana's furry neck as she sobbed into the soft fur.

He fought the desire to go to her, hold her, try to comfort her. Afraid of intruding where he wasn't wanted, instead he closed the door and once again leaned his head against it, his heart crying along with his ex-wife for the little boy who loved Susan and had left behind a half-eaten Twinkie.

THERESA CRIED until she felt there was no more moisture left in her body. Funny, that it had taken a simple blue backpack to completely undo her. Still, the tears were cathartic, and when she was finished with them, she felt a renewed burst of strength rally inside her.

Here in Eric's bed, she felt close to him. It was a spiritual closeness that had no basis in reality, but offered comfort nonetheless. His little-boy scent clung to the sheets and pillowcase, and Theresa breathed in and held her breath, as if capturing Eric's essence deep within her.

The breath whooshed out of her as the dog jumped up on her chest and licked her face. "Hey!" she protested, a sudden burst of laughter bubbling to her lips.

Sitting up, she scrubbed the dog behind his ears, smiling as he gazed at her with adoring eyes. Leave it to Sully to get Eric a dog without thought of checking it with her. What had he called the mutt? Oh, yes...Montana.

"Montana." The dog barked as she said his name aloud. "Oh, Eric is going to love you." He barked again, almost looking as though he were smiling. Theresa gave him another quick hug, then stood. "Come on, let's go find you something to eat."

The moment she left the bedroom, she heard the raised voices coming from the kitchen. "Dammit, Donny, don't cut me out," Sully's voice rang out, filled with frustration and undercurrents of rich anger. Montana growled, as if unsettled by the tension.

Theresa patted the dog reassuringly, then entered the kitchen, where the two men stood facing each other, both of their faces twisted with stress. "What's going on?" she asked.

"They found Burt Neiman," Sully said, his gaze not leaving Donny.

Theresa's heart leaped. "Was...was Eric with him?"

"No. They found him a couple hours ago in a Clinton motel room with a hooker. I'm on my way to the station now to interview both Burt and his lady friend," Donny explained.

"Let me come with you," Sully said.

"Dammit, Sully, you want me to lose my job?" Donny exploded. "I already bent the rules so you and Theresa could talk to Roger at the jail. Don't put me in an awkward position."

"But I'll make sure Burt tells the truth," Sully protested, equally loud. Montana barked raucously, as if needing to add his voice to the din.

Donny raked a hand through his hair as Theresa settled the dog. "Sorry, Sully. No go. You can't interview possible suspects. You aren't a cop anymore."

"Sully." Theresa placed a hand on his arm, seeing the torment in his eyes, knowing the impotent helplessness that roared inside him. "Would you help me decorate the tree? Remember? You said you would help."

He looked down at her, the blaze of anger subsiding as a deep, abiding weariness took its place. "The tree?" He looked at her blankly, as if he'd forgotten it was Christmas and a bare pine tree stood waiting in the corner of the living room.

"The Christmas tree. We need to decorate it for when Eric gets home."

"Yeah...right. Of course I'll help." He looked

back at Donny. "You'll call if there's any information...any news at all?"

"You know I will," Donny replied. He motioned for Sully to walk with him out the back door. While they were gone, Theresa found two bowls that would serve as makeshift food and water dishes for Montana. She filled the water bowl and set it on the floor.

As Montana drank, she wandered to the window and peered out to where Sully and Donny seemed to be in the middle of another argument. *Be careful, Sully,* she thought to herself. *Don't anger the people who are trying to help.*

It was the waiting that was killing them. Each shrill ring of the phone sliced off a piece of their heart, heightened tension and caused nerves to reach their breaking point.

She felt like a prisoner here in her home, afraid to leave, afraid she'd miss a phone call, a clue...something that would bring Eric back to her.

At least by decorating the tree, they'd be doing something...something besides sitting and staring out the window, or looking into one another's eyes and seeing a hopeless despair reflected there.

She frowned and turned away from the window, wondering if Sully and Donny were arguing about something really important or if they were merely releasing tension, bickering to let off pressure.

She jumped as Sully came through the door, slamming it behind him. "Dammit, I should be down there talking to that creep!" he exclaimed.

"But you know that's not possible," Theresa

countered. She sighed. "Oh, Sully, we can't take chances. If Burt had something to do with Eric's disappearance, you wouldn't want to do something that would jeopardize a case against him."

"I suppose you're right," he replied grudgingly. He leaned against the front door, as if too weary to move.

"Is that what you and Donny were fighting about just now?" He shook his head, and Theresa frowned, suddenly realizing how silent the house was around them. "Where is everyone?"

"That's what Donny and I were fighting about," Sully replied. He paced across the confines of the kitchen, from one end to the other, then back again. "He has to pull most of the men from this."

"Why?" Theresa asked, her voice plaintive and higher-pitched than usual.

Sully paced the length of the kitchen once again, then stopped just in front of her. Stepping close, he placed his palms on either side of her, framing her face, much as Robert had done earlier in the morning. "Right now, Eric is nothing more than a missing kid...possibly a runaway."

"You know that's not true. Eric would never run away," she protested, oddly comforted by the familiar feel of his large, strong hands against her skin.

"You know that, and I know that, but without a ransom demand, the police can't discount the possibility that Eric ran away or got lost. And Donny can't justify all the manpower on this one case."

"So then what happens now? The police just forget that somewhere out there is a little nine-year-old boy who for some reason can't get back home?" She wanted to rant, she wanted to rave over this new bit of information, but she didn't want to move away from Sully's touch. His fingers were warm, easing somewhat the icy winds of fear that had blown through her since the moment she discovered Eric hadn't made it to school yesterday morning.

"Donny will still be in charge of the case, and he'll continue to work it, with probably half a dozen men. But it won't be the priority case for all the officers, like it was in the initial hours of the search."

"Are they giving up?" she asked, the question easing out of her on a painful breath.

"No." He dropped his hands from her face. "But crime in this city hasn't stopped because Eric is missing. There was a murder on the south side of town a few hours ago, and two armed robberies in the past eight hours. When I was on the force, we used to talk about the fact that the holidays bring out the worst in some people."

She sighed, his words producing a cold wind that blew straight through to her core. "Come on, Sully. Let's decorate the tree. At the moment, it's the only thing we can do for our son." She grabbed his hand, and together they went into the living room.

It took them several minutes to get the boxes of decorations from shelves in various closets. Then, as Sully worked to string the lights, Theresa unpacked the box of ornaments they'd collected during their married life.

It felt odd, to be working on the tree with no joy in her heart, without the sound of carols playing on the stereo, the pungent scent of spiced cider filling the air.

It felt even odder to be decorating the tree with Sully. She'd believed it was something that would never happen again. She'd reconciled herself to Christmases without his presence, just as she'd adjusted to lonely nights in her solitary bed.

She sat back and watched as Sully untangled a string of lights, his brow furrowed in concentration. She'd never believed much in love before Sully. As the eldest of four children, it had been up to Theresa to hold her family together when her father walked out on them, when she was fifteen.

Theresa had watched her mother fall apart, her sisters draw into shells of hurt and bewilderment. She'd become the strong one, holding the family together, and she'd decided then that she would never give a man that kind of power over her. Until the day she met Sullivan Mathews.

She'd just moved from her family home back east to Kansas City, to take a job in the prosecutor's office. Sully had been the state witness on her very first case. She'd taken one look into his ash-colored eyes, felt the power in his slow, devastating smile, and known her life would never be the same again.

They'd been married six months later. She'd given all she had to give to Sully...but it hadn't been enough. Resentment bubbled up in her chest as she once again gazed at him. The one time she decided to trust a man with her heart, he'd cast it aside like a pair of worn pants.

Never again, she promised herself as she once again focused on unwrapping the ornaments. Never again would she allow a man to get so close, to own her heart so completely. The heartbreak Sully had left behind was tremendous enough to last a lifetime.

"You should have asked me about the dog," she said as she looked over to where Montana was stretched out on the sofa, as if he'd lived here forever.

"I figured if you wouldn't let Eric keep him, then Montana could stay at my place and Eric could see him on the weekends," Sully replied as he spiraled lights around the tree.

"And I'd be the bad guy," Theresa replied irritably.

Sully paused and looked at her, the wrinkle back in his brow. "Is there a reason why you're attempting to pick a fight with me?"

"I'm not—" Theresa flushed, realizing that was exactly what she'd been trying to do. "Maybe I am," she admitted, although she wasn't about to confess that she needed to feel anger toward him in order to guard her heart against other, unwanted feelings where he was concerned.

He put the lights down and walked over to where she sat on the floor. Hunkering down beside her, he smiled—the first real smile she'd seen from him since he arrived at her house. The same slow, catastrophic smile that always made her heart skip a beat and her pulse race. "It's a natural instinct, I think."

She looked at him curiously. "What is?"

"The need to fight, to fill yourself with anger to mask the fear."

"You preferred drinking to fighting to mask whatever it was you felt." It was a blow below the belt, and she saw the impact of the verbal punch in the narrowing of his eyes, the soft intake of his breath. He stood up and walked back to where he'd been working.

Theresa knew she should apologize, but the words had been said more to remind herself of what they'd gone through than in an effort to hurt him. Still, shame coursed through her.

His brief bout of drinking had always been a taboo topic between them. At first, Theresa had thought he drank to ease the physical pain the bullet had left behind. But eventually she had had to face the cold, hard truth, that he drank to endure the unhappiness of their marriage. He'd stopped drinking almost immediately after he left her.

"Theresa, I'm not going to fight with you, no matter what you say to try to get under my skin." He finished hanging the lights and began arranging gold garland on the boughs. "Our son is missing, and if we can't help each other get through it, then we belittle the love that produced him. We mock the years we spent together. I'll fight with Donny, and all the personnel in the police department, if that's what it takes to save Eric. But I won't fight with you. I just can't.''

Theresa stared down at the ornament in her hand. She and Sully had bought it for Eric's sixth Christmas. It was a little red bicycle...just like the one that had been under the tree on Christmas morning. ''You remember this?'' She held it up, offering a smile as truce.

''How could I forget it?'' He returned her smile—a gesture of forgiveness that made her grateful. ''I was up until two in the morning putting together the bicycle we gave to Eric that year.'' He finished arranging the garland and crouched down next to her amid the ornaments that chronicled their life together.

They took turns hanging the baubles on the tree, each one evoking a specific memory to be savored. And each memory of Eric nourished Theresa's inner strength, fed the belief that somehow Eric would find his way back home to the parents who loved him.

''The phone has been quiet for a while now,'' Theresa said as they dripped long pieces of tinsel on the branches.

''Yeah, Donny told the reporters out front to let their colleagues know that whoever called and tied up the line would be arrested for obstruction of justice.''

Theresa looked at Sully in surprise. ''Can he do that?''

Sully smiled. ''Probably not, but as long as the press thinks he can, they'll abide by his wishes.'' He bent down and gently picked up the ornate porcelain-faced angel, with her featherlike wings.

"No," Theresa cried as he reached up to place her in her heavenly perch atop the tree. "No, please... Remember, that's Eric's job." Every year Sully had lifted Eric up so that he could be the one to set the angel in place as the finishing touch to their tree.

Sully's eyes darkened with pain, and he returned the angel to her box of tissue. "You're right," he said softly. "We'll wait and let Eric put her where she belongs." He plugged in the lights, and the tree came aglow, as if a physical manifestation of their hope, their faith.

Instinctively they moved together, Sully's arm wrapping around her shoulders as she leaned into him. The beauty of the tree almost made her shiver, but the emptiness at the very top caused a lump to form in her throat.

"It's beautiful, isn't it?" Sully tightened his arm around her. "But it's not right. And it won't be right until he's home."

Theresa closed her eyes, wanting to tell Sully that nothing had been right since the moment he left her. But she couldn't put that on him, couldn't burden him with her weakness. And God help her, but Sully had always been her weakness.

She wanted him to be happy, even if his happiness was dependent on a life without her. Still, she was grateful that he was here for her now.

Without him, she would stop being strong. Without him, she'd fall apart, lose her mind, plunge into a deep, black hole that would swallow her up.

"We'll get through this, Sully," she said, turning so that she stood directly in front of him. She reached her arms up and locked her hands behind his neck.

Gazing into his soot-colored eyes, with their sinfully long, dark lashes, she thought she saw a spark of something she'd never thought she'd see again in his eyes.

Beneath the worry, beyond the disquiet, desire flared. He tightened his grip on her waist, tugging her closer against the solid warmth of his body. His breath was warm and sweet on her face as he looked down at her.

"Sully?" She wasn't sure what question she was asking, and in any case he had no reply. The nebulous expression she'd thought was desire disappeared, shuttered behind blankness as he released his hold on her.

"Theresa..." An explosion at the window interrupted whatever he intended to say. Glass flew inward as the window shattered.

Sully yanked Theresa to the floor, covering her body with his. For a long moment, neither of them moved, the only sound the howl of the frigid wind that suddenly filled the room.

"What...what happened?" Theresa finally whispered.

"I don't know.... I think somebody wanted to get our attention." Sully stood and held out a hand to help Theresa up. "There." He pointed to a brick on the floor just beneath the window, amid glittering shards of glass.

"What is it?"

Theresa watched as Sully carefully dusted glass pieces from the brick, then picked it up. An ordinary red brick, a rubber band holding a piece of paper around its middle.

She held her breath as Sully pulled off the rubber band, then opened the sheet of paper, his hands trembling. He scanned the contents briefly, then looked at her, his gaze cold and hard. "We've finally got our ransom demand."

Chapter Seven

Sully held the ransom note with two fingers, although he suspected he didn't need to worry about smudging fingerprints. Whoever sent it had probably been smart enough to wear gloves while preparing it.

He read it carefully two times, the first time his mind working like a cop's. Plain paper. Block letters. Impossible to trace. Dammit.

The second time he read it, his mind worked like a father's. Horror swept through him, chilling him, as the frigid wintry air cascaded through the window.

"What does it say?" Theresa's voice was hoarse as she moved next to him. Montana whined, and she absently leaned down and scratched his head.

"It says for you to take a paper sack filled with twenty-five thousand dollars to the Pineridge mall tomorrow afternoon at two. You're to place it in a trash can in front of Dillards, on the first level. The bills are to be small, nonsequential and nontraceable. No cops. No tricks."

"Do you think—" Whatever Theresa had been about to say was interrupted by the shrill ring of the phone. She and Sully froze. As the phone rang a second time, Sully pulled her into the kitchen, where he turned on the recording equipment and gestured for Theresa to answer.

"You got my note?" The strange voice filled the kitchen.

Theresa's eyes flickered to Sully's. "Yes," she breathed.

"If I see a cop, the boy dies. If you jerk me around, the boy dies. Do as you're told and he'll be all right."

Sully wanted to crawl through the receiver and follow the wires to the monster at the other end of the line. Instead, he quickly scribbled several words on a pad, then held it up for Theresa to read.

"How...how do I know you have Eric?" she asked, reading Sully's question.

There was a long pause. "Blue jeans. Blue sweater and a Chiefs jacket. I got him...and if you want him back, you'll do as you're told. Follow your instructions." A click...then the sound of dead air.

"Wait!" Theresa cried, but it was too late. The caller had hung up.

"I've got to contact Donny," Sully said as Theresa sank into a chair at the table. "Dammit, wouldn't you know we'd be contacted when nobody else was here?"

"Can't you tell where the call came from? Send Donny with a bunch of men to the address where the call was made?" Theresa asked.

Sully looked at the caller ID box and frowned. "A

pay phone. And I'll just bet a check of the phone will yield nothing, not even a partial fingerprint of the caller.'' He picked up the phone and dialed the number of the station. ''Let me speak to Lieutenant Holbrook,'' he said tersely to whoever answered the phone at the station.

As he waited for Donny to get to the phone, he thought again of that voice. It had sounded like the embodiment of evil. Without emotion, without passion.

''Holbrook isn't available at the moment.''

Sully tightened his grip on the phone. ''This is Sullivan Mathews. My kid is missing, and we just got a ransom demand. You find Holbrook and make him available.''

''He's en route to your house now.''

Sully slammed down the phone, the force of his action making Theresa jump. ''He's on his way here,'' he explained. Cold. The house was cold. Or maybe it was just him. Cold to the bones. Cold to the soul.

''That voice. Something wasn't right. It didn't sound human,'' Theresa said.

Sully nodded. ''The caller used a voice synthesizer or something to alter it.''

There was no way to tell for sure if the ransom demand had been a hoax, or the real thing. One thing was certain. Sully hoped if it was true, he got just one minute...one second...alone with whoever had taken his son, whoever had orchestrated this horror.

''You have any plywood around here?'' he asked.

Theresa looked at him blankly. She looked dazed, unfocused. Sully wondered if the phone call had shoved her into shock. "Plywood?" she finally echoed.

He pulled her up from the kitchen chair and led her into the living room, where the temperature had dropped some twenty degrees and the wind whistled through the broken glass of the window.

He needed to keep her moving, needed to take her mind off the call, the horrible possibilities. "We need to fix the window, Theresa."

She looked at the window, then appeared to pull herself together. She shrugged her shoulders, as if casting off a heavy shroud. "Of course...the window. There are some scraps of plywood in the garage."

"I'll get the plywood. Why don't you clean up that glass?"

She nodded, and Sully left the living room. Once in the garage, he sat down at the workbench, needing a moment to summon strength. If the call had not been a hoax, then now they knew. Eric wasn't lost. He hadn't fallen in a ditch and broken a leg. Somebody had him. Somebody was holding him against his will.

The bicycle Sully had spent hours putting together several Christmases ago stood in the corner. The chrome and paint shone like new, not a speck of dirt or mud to mar the appearance. Eric was a good kid. He took care of his things.

That was why Sully had decided to get him Montana. Theresa wouldn't have to remind him to feed the dog, or clean up a mess. Eric was unusually responsible for his age. Such a good kid.

Tears burned at Sully's eyes. He drew in deep gulps of air in an effort to stymie them, but it was no use. As he thought of his son's sturdy little body, the scent of boyhood that always clung to him, Sully lost it.

His tears oozed from his eyes, trekking down his cheeks, as he stood in the center of the garage and stared at the bicycle.

The tears made him angry. Another sign of weakness. Another character flaw. He swiped at them angrily, then grabbed a hammer and a handful of nails from the workbench.

By the time he found a piece of plywood the right size, his tears had stopped. Instead, a cold hard ball of anger sat in his chest. He welcomed the anger, found it easier to accept than tears. Besides, he didn't want Theresa to see his weakness.

When he returned to the living room, Theresa stood in front of the window, blood running from the tip of one of her fingers. "Theresa!" He dropped the wood and rushed to her side, realized instantly that she'd cut herself while cleaning up the broken glass.

Taking her arm, he led her into the kitchen and toward the sink. He turned on the cold water and pulled her hand beneath the gentle flow. "It doesn't look too bad," he said. "I don't think there's any glass in it." With a paper towel, he dried the wound. "You have any bandages?"

She nodded. "In the drawer by the sink."

He found them and placed one over the cut. "Okay?" he asked.

She looked at him, her eyes open wounds of pain. "No. No, I'm not all right."

He pulled her to him. She seemed to meld into him, her body fitting perfectly against his. He closed his eyes, smelling the sweetness of her hair, her body heat warming his.

"I keep wondering why this has happened to us. What did we do wrong?"

"We didn't do anything wrong," Sully said as he tightened his arms around her. "You can't think that way. Sometimes bad things happen to good people."

She leaned away from him so that she could look into his eyes. "Yes, they do, don't they? Just like the night you got shot."

"That was different." He released her. "Come on, let's get that plywood up before it gets any colder in here."

He felt her gaze on his face, studying him, knew she'd never understood about that night he was shot. She hadn't understood, because Sully hadn't told her about his suspicions, and he'd certainly never confessed the residual fear that tormented him after that night.

It took them only a few minutes to fix the window. "You'll need to have somebody come out and replace this pane," he said as he hammered in the last nail. "But I imagine you won't be able to get anyone out until after the holidays."

They both turned as Donny flew in the front door. "I heard you got a demand," he said without preamble.

Sully nodded and gestured toward the note, which lay open on the end table. He watched as Donny carefully picked it up by the corner and read it. "We also got a call," Sully said when Donny had finished reading the note.

"You get it on tape?"

Sully nodded, and the three of them went into the kitchen, where the tape of the caller was played over and over again.

"What happens now?" Theresa asked.

Donny sank down to the table. "We probably need to turn this over to the FBI."

"No..." The word shot out of Sully. He didn't want the federal boys in on this...not yet. He knew the police department were his friends, would do whatever it took to get Eric back safe and sound. If the FBI entered into the scenario, then they could all find themselves bound up with red tape and bureaucracy. "Not yet." He looked at Theresa, then at Donny. "There's no guarantee this ransom demand is legit. We don't know for sure that Eric has been kidnapped."

"But the caller knew what clothes he was wearing," Theresa protested.

"He could have picked up that information off the newscasts," Donny explained. He looked back at Sully. "You know I can't encourage you to meet that ransom demand."

"But of course we're going to pay it," Theresa replied. "We're going to do exactly what the caller told us to do. We can't take a chance by not doing that."

Sully could tell by Theresa's voice that he didn't dare oppose her on this. As a cop, he knew it was never wise to play a kidnapper's game. As a father...he'd jump through hoops to get his son back.

"Then we set up a sting. If we're going to get this guy, it will have to be at the drop," Donny said.

"No!" Theresa looked first at Donny, then at Sully. "You heard what he said. No cops. We can't take a chance. We have to do what he said." There was an edge of hysteria in her voice.

"Theresa, I promise you we'll make sure this guy doesn't see a cop. He won't know we're there, but we can't let him take the money and run. The risk is too great." Donny turned and looked at Sully. "Can you get the money?"

"Somehow...some way, we'll get the money," Sully answered, although he wasn't sure how. He and Theresa had never managed to get together much of a savings account, and his paychecks from his job as a bouncer weren't exactly terrific.

"Robert." Theresa looked at Sully. "Robert will get us the money. I'll call him right now." She disappeared into the living room, leaving the two men alone in the kitchen.

"This isn't about the money." Sully frowned and rubbed a hand across his forehead, where it felt as if a metal band were slowly tightening.

"What do you mean?"

Sully looked at Donny. "Think about it. Twenty-five thousand dollars is a pathetically paltry amount for a kidnapper to request. Why not a million...half a million? If you're going to go to all the trouble and risk of kidnapping a kid, why do it for twenty-five g's?"

"So, if it's not about the money...what's it all about?"

"I don't know." Sully pinched the bridge of his nose, his headache now pounding with nauseating intensity. "It could be a hoax...somebody hoping to cash in on a hot news story. At least we know it isn't Burt Neiman."

"What makes you say that?"

"Wasn't he in custody for questioning?"

Donny frowned. "Yeah, but we couldn't hold him. He was released about two hours ago. He would have had plenty of time to throw that brick and make the call."

Theresa came back in the room. "Robert is going to bring the money by first thing in the morning." Sully noticed that some of the fear had left her eyes. "It's going to be all right," she said, as much to herself as to anyone else. She sank down at the table across from Sully and reached for his hand across the table. "We'll give him the money and he'll give us back Eric. It's going to be just fine, isn't it?"

Sully nodded wearily. He didn't have the heart to tell her they couldn't trust the word of a kidnapper.

ANOTHER NIGHT of darkness. Another night without her baby. Theresa sat alone in the deepening shadows of her bedroom, trying to fill the emptiness with thoughts of Eric.

She'd been in labor with him for nearly twenty hours...excruciatingly hard labor...and yet the moment he was born and the doctor placed him on her chest, she'd magically forgotten those hours of pain. Instead, she'd been filled with a love so intense, so profound, she wept with joy.

As he lay there on the warmth of her breasts, his bright blue eyes had looked at her with ancient wisdom, as if in the instant after birth he still retained all the secrets of the universe. Then he'd blinked, and that wisdom had faded away and he'd been just a baby. Her baby. His arms had flailed and he'd begun to cry and she had wondered if he cried because his prebirth memories and knowledge had seeped away, leaving him frightened and helpless in a brand-new world. At that moment, Theresa had fully understood the meaning of the maternal bond.

Flashes of Eric filled her head, memories rich in clarity and texture. The smell of his skin after a bath, the silky softness of his hair, the feel of his hand in hers, so small, so trusting.

The winter he was three, she and Sully had bundled him up in a snowsuit and taken him out into the snow, where he'd promptly gotten stuck in a snowdrift. She closed her eyes, her mind filled with the vision. She could see clearly the look of surprise on his face when he'd realized he couldn't move his legs. His blue eyes had flashed in consternation, his cheeks had reddened like ripened apples, and he'd raised his arms to her for help. She'd picked him up and promptly lost her footing, tumbling backward into the drift.

And Sully. She remembered Sully, his cheeks ruddy from the cold, his rich laughter warming her throughout as he helped them out of the drift.

She squeezed her eyes tightly closed, the memory of Eric's giggles, of Sully's laughter, filling her heart. She tried to hang on to the pleasant memory...but the harder she fought to retain it, the more elusive it became, until it finally disappeared and she was once again a frightened woman sitting in a darkened bedroom while her husband sat in the kitchen with several police officers, plotting strategy for a ransom-demand payoff.

"Be safe, Eric," she whispered. "Dear God, keep him safe until tomorrow, when he can come home." Surely if they paid the ransom, the kidnapper would release Eric. Surely the man knew he held her heart, her very soul, in his hands.

"Theresa?" Sully walked into the room. He closed the door behind him and sat down next to her on the bed. "You should get some sleep."

"So should you," she countered, noting how the flickering Christmas lights outside the window splashed their brilliant colors across his tired countenance. "I was just thinking about Eric," she said, grateful when Sully put an arm around her. She leaned into him and sighed against the front of his shirt.

"What about him?" he asked softly, his hand raising up to caress the length of her hair down her back.

"You remember how when he was little he'd call butterflies 'flutterbys'? And the way he'd make up stories before he could read? He'd look at the pictures in his books and make up things to go along with the pictures. And how he loves the rain because he says it washes the whole world clean and makes it smell nice?"

She turned in his arms so that she was facing him, and placed her hands on either side of his face. She could feel the slight roughness of day's-end whiskers on his cheeks. "He's the best of us both, isn't he?" she asked.

He nodded, and in the depths of his eyes she saw need...the aching need of a man in torment, whose only hope for comfort existed in her arms. "Oh, Sully," she said softly, then kissed him.

The instant her lips touched his, passion flared inside her, hot and raging out of control. She tasted his response, as hot and desperate as her own.

Together they fell back on the bed, their mouths still locked as they drew strength and gave comfort to one another. Hungrily their tongues flicked and swirled around each other, needing passion to usurp fear, desire to replace uncertainty. They wanted to lose themselves in each other, momentarily forgetting their heartbreak, their fear.

"Make love to me, Sully," Theresa gasped when the breathless kiss finally ended.

"Theresa...I..." Indecision darkened his eyes. Theresa knew he was allowing rational thought to gain hold. She didn't want that. She wanted irrational thought, mind-numbing emotion.

"I need you, Sully," she whispered as her hands worked the buttons on his shirt. She splayed her hands across the warmth of his bare chest, and he groaned...a groan of surrender.

This time it was his lips that captured hers, stealing her breath, then giving it back to her, as his hands caressed up and down her back, tangled in her hair, evoking flames wherever he touched. Within minutes, his passion was huge, leaving no room for thought, no place for anything but this moment in time.

She surrendered utterly to him, aching with the need to assuage the emptiness that gnawed at her insides, allowing need to engulf her, in a momentary respite of mindless alienation from painful emotions of fear for her son.

Pushing his shirt off his shoulders, her hands caressed his broad chest, exploring the familiar contours of hard muscle dusted with wiry hair. At the same time, he pulled at the bottom of her sweatshirt, tugging it upward, over her head. He threw it across the room, then unsnapped her jeans.

"Wait..." She moved off the bed and stood, quickly removing the rest of her clothing. He did the same, his eyes glittering darkly as they lingered on her.

The first frenzied flood of passion passed as they stared at each other in the semidarkness of the room. She knew Sully didn't move toward her because he was giving her a chance to change her mind, to call a halt to their lovemaking before it progressed any further. And that caring only made her want him more.

She moved toward him...against him...gasping as her naked flesh made intimate contact with his. Oh, she'd forgotten. She'd forgotten the exquisite joy of naked flesh upon naked flesh, of heat meeting heat, soft need melding with hard hunger.

She'd forgotten the beauty she always found in making love with Sully. Even though they had been separated for nearly a year, it had been much longer since they made love. The physical aspect of their relationship had died on the night of Sully's shooting.

As she pressed her body against his, she felt the rapid beating of his heart, the hardness of his desire pressed against her thigh. With a deep, almost guttural moan, he wrapped his arms around her, his lips seeking the flesh of her neck, the secret erogenous place behind her ear.

"Theresa...sweet Theresa," he whispered as his hands cupped her buttocks and drew her more intimately against him.

"Love me, Sully. Love me like you used to."

He swept her up in his arms and carried her to the

bed. Sully had always liked a slov' pace when making love, and this night was no different.

He stroked her body in long, fluid motions, kissed her in the intimate places he knew evoked the most pleasure, until she trembled with urgency. Still he held back, taking her to heights she'd never reached, loving her as she feared she'd never be loved again.

When he finally entered her, she cried out his name, clutching his shoulders and meeting his thrusts with frantic need.

Together they climbed...higher...faster...until they climaxed, each crying out the other's name.

Afterward, Sully watched her sleep. She'd fallen asleep almost immediately, as if their lovemaking had used up the last of her reservoir of strength.

He stifled the impulse to reach out and stroke the rich darkness of her hair, not wanting to bother her sleep. If she could find some modicum of peace in the oblivion of sleep, then he didn't want to disrupt it.

He rolled over on his back, watching the blinking outside Christmas lights seeping through the curtains to paint colorful patterns on the ceiling.

He'd forgotten the pleasure of making love with Theresa, forgotten how completely she gave of herself to him, how sweetly she surrendered. But he wasn't fool enough to read anything into this particular night of lovemaking.

She'd needed him to sweep away her heartsickness. Just as he'd needed her. When Eric was back home and things returned to normal, he and Theresa would resume their separate lives.

He both eagerly awaited and dreaded the coming of the next day. If they paid the ransom, would Eric be returned to them unharmed? Was it a real demand...or the work of a crackpot? Who was behind this? If the motive wasn't money, then what?

God, there were so many questions...so few answers. Without motive, it was almost impossible to guess who might have Eric. And if the motive was strictly money, it could be anyone.

He slid from the bed and padded to the window. Staring out into the purple shadows of dusk, he wondered what they had missed.... What clues had they overlooked? Who hated him or Theresa enough to do this? Or was it possible Eric had simply been a random pick?

Making a decision, he grabbed his pants and tugged them on, then grabbed his shirt. He fastened each button methodically, thinking back over everything that had happened since he heard about Eric's disappearance.

It was time he started thinking like a cop, not like a father...time to stop taking everyone else's word for things and investigate on his own. And he knew exactly where he intended to start. Donny might have had to walk on eggshells with Burt Neiman, because of his badge and the responsibilities that came with it. Sully had no such restrictions. He wasn't a cop anymore.

ERIC WATCHED the coming of night through the narrow cracks around the boards at the window. He didn't want it to be night again.

He'd spent the morning reading the comic books that had been in the bag, then eaten one of the sandwiches and taken a nap.

After he awakened, he'd tried to pry the boards off the window. He'd worked and worked, until his fingers ached and he'd broken two nails. He'd finally managed to release one side of one board. It wasn't enough to let him climb out the window, but it was a start.

If the police didn't come to rescue him tonight, then tomorrow he'd work on prying off the boards again. Sooner or later he'd make a space big enough to wiggle through.

He stared at the window, where the last flickering light faded with every breath he took. The dark scared him, but he would be all right if he just thought of stuff.

He curled up on the bed and closed his eyes, then drew a picture of his mom in his mind. Even though she was his mother, he thought she was one of the prettiest women in the whole world. He liked the way her nose wrinkled when she laughed, how her hair smelled when she gave him a hug. Her blue eyes were the color of the sky, and they almost always twinkled and danced. He held on to the vision of her until it hurt and he felt the burn of tears behind his eyes.

He missed his dad, too. His dad was the strongest,

greatest guy in the whole world. Eric remembered the time his dad had come to his class to talk about being a policeman. Eric had been so proud.

Even a bad guy's bullet couldn't kill his dad. Eric thought his dad might be related to Superman. Maybe a cousin or something.

He also missed the smell of his classroom, and Bobby Johnson's goofy laugh. He missed his hamster, Petey, who sometimes bit him but never too hard.

The one thing he didn't miss was his poster of Joe Montana. And he didn't miss it because he knew Joe was here in the cellar with him, whispering in his ear, telling him it was going to be all right. And Eric believed Joe. He'd seen the films of the old football games where Joe had pulled miracles in the fourth quarter of a game with mere seconds left. Joe was the miracle man, and next to his dad, Joe was the bestest hero in the world.

Yes, Eric believed in Joe, and he believed in miracles. He pulled his legs up tighter against his chest, wishing for a blanket to keep him warm and a night-light to chase away the dark. He could use one of those miracles any time now.

Chapter Eight

Sully left the house and got into his car. Before starting the engine, he checked the glove box to make sure his gun was still inside. He'd stowed it there before going into Theresa's, knowing the sight of the gun would frighten her.

For nearly an hour, he drove aimlessly, letting thoughts and feelings about Eric's case roll around in his head. He still had the feeling that the kidnapping had little to do with money. And that left only revenge as a motivation. The problem was, he didn't know if the revenge was targeted at him or at Theresa.

As a prosecutor, Theresa worked in a job that made her a target for the unsavory, the unscrupulous. As an ex-cop, Sully had the same liability.

He wondered if the kidnapper had been watching Theresa's house. The brick and the phone call had both occurred while the police were absent. Coincidence? Sully didn't believe in coincidence.

The idea of some creep watching the house made his skin crawl, not for himself, but for Theresa. He tightened his grip on the steering wheel and focused on where he was headed, what he intended to do.

He drove to Sam's Pit and parked in the lot, surprised to find a big crowd at the bar. Didn't these people have homes? Families? That was where he should be...at home with his family.

He turned off the engine and got out of the car. But, of course, that was impossible. He no longer had his wife...and his son had been kidnapped.

He was met at the door by Sam Walker, the bar's owner. "Hey, Sully. Heard about your son." The big man clapped Sully on the back, his meaty mug softened by sympathy. "Did they find him yet?"

Sully shook his head. "Can I use your phone, Sam?"

"Sure...sure, whatever you need." Sam led Sully through the bar, the noise inside a raucous cacophony of chaos. Sully followed his boss through a doorway at the right of the wooden bar and into a small office, where the noise was muted and the desk lamp a pleasant glow.

Sam gestured to the telephone. "Take whatever time you need. I just wish there was something else I could do."

"This is fine." Sully shook the man's hand. Sam was a decent man, and Sully knew he had a wife and three children of his own.

Moments later, alone in the office, Sully picked up the phone and dialed Kip's number. Kip answered on the second ring.

"I need a favor," Sully said without preamble.

"What?"

"I want Burt Neiman's address."

Sully's words were met with a long pause. "Sully, that's not a good idea. Holbrook already interviewed him, and he didn't seem to know anything about Eric."

"Yeah, well, I need to be certain of that."

"Sully...for God's sakes, leave it to the cops on the case. Let them take care of things."

"Like they took care of the investigation of the night I got shot?" Sully returned sharply. Kip was one of the few men who had a hint of what Sully suspected about that night so long ago. "I have to do something, Kip. It's my son we're talking about."

Kip sighed. "It will take me a few minutes to get the information."

"You can call me at this number." Sully gave him the number of the phone he was using.

"Where are you?" Kip asked.

"At the Pit. I couldn't very well make this call from home. Donny would have me arrested if he knew I intended to talk to Burt."

"You'd be safer in a jail cell," Kip replied dryly. "I'll call you when I've got what you want."

"Thanks, Kip, you're a good friend."

"No, I'm crazy as a loon to be doing this." Without another word, Kip hung up.

Sully sank into the chair behind the desk, the headache that had plagued him earlier back once again. Rubbing his forehead, he thought back to those moments when Theresa had been in his arms.

It had been heaven to hold her again, to smell the sweetness of her fragrance, to taste her mouth, her skin. It had been the first time in eighteen months that he felt right, as if he were finally home.

It had been a moment of peace in the eye of a storm. A brief respite from the loneliness, the isolation, that had become his life.

But he knew he couldn't go back...couldn't resume a life with Theresa. He wouldn't put himself in a position where he might someday see disgust in her eyes, or pity. She was a strong woman who deserved a strong man, not a man tormented by nightmares, scarred from a bullet and afraid that eventually he'd lose himself in a bottle of booze.

Funny, that through all this, the greatest test he'd ever been through, he'd had no desire to drink. He wanted only one thing. His son back, safe from harm. And he knew that if he was going to help accomplish that, he had to remain clearheaded.

He had no doubt Kip would get him the information. Kip was a good cop, but his real talent was in accessing the Internet via his home computer. Kip had the skill of a magician when it came to getting into private areas, somehow maneuvering around password demands.

He jumped as the phone rang, and snatched up the receiver. "Yeah."

"Thirty-two-forty-nine Autumn Drive," Kip said.

Sully frowned. He knew the area. Upper-class neighborhood. "Pretty fancy address for a street punk."

"It's the parents' address. Both of them lived at home. A couple of slugs who apparently have more money than sense."

"I owe you, Kip."

"No, you don't. This conversation never happened." Once again, Kip disconnected.

Sully left the bar immediately. It was almost nine, and he hoped to catch the young man at home before he went out for the night.

When he reached the Neiman house, a souped-up Chevy sat in the driveway, along with a brand-new pickup and a BMW. Sully had a feeling the Chevy belonged to Burt...the other vehicles to his parents.

Playing a hunch, Sully remained in his car, parked across the street from the Neiman residence. He had a feeling that if he was patient, he wouldn't have to disturb the elder Neimans. Burt would come out for a night of play, and Sully would be waiting.

As the minutes ticked by, becoming half an hour, then forty-five minutes, Sully wondered if he'd played the wrong hunch. Perhaps the car wasn't Burt's at all. Or maybe the young man, after spending several hours at the police station, didn't feel like going out tonight.

An hour later, Sully's hunch paid off as the quarry left the house. He carried a paper bag in one hand and whistled merrily as he got into the Chevy.

Sully's initial impulse was to question Burt outside his home, but as the young man pulled out of the driveway, Sully waited a moment, then followed him.

They drove through the center of town, Sully keeping enough distance between the two cars that, hopefully, Burt wouldn't realize he was being followed.

They left the city limits and drove another five miles or so before Burt turned off on a narrow dirt road that led to an abandoned shanty. Sully didn't make the turn, but instead pulled his car to the side of the road and killed the engine and lights.

He grabbed his gun and shoved it into his waistband, then got out of his car and hid behind a stand of brush. The cold wind sliced through him, but he hardly felt it as he focused on the Chevy.

The car came to a halt in front of the shanty, and Burt got out and disappeared into the small wood structure. The small glow of some kind of light spilled out from the cracks and crevices.

What in the hell was going on? What was Burt doing out here in the middle of nowhere? Adrenaline swept through Sully. Was it possible Eric was in that shanty? Tied up...prone on the floor? Isolated and forgotten, it was a perfect place to stash a kidnap victim.

Pulling his gun from his waistband, Sully advanced on the dilapidated building, his heart pounding a thunderous rhythm in his chest.

The night was dark, the moon spilling down just enough light for Sully to advance cautiously. He crept from one stand of brush to another, approaching the shanty with the stealth of a wary animal.

Even though you have a gun in your hand, you

won't be able to use it, a small voice whispered in his head. *You'll freeze. Just like you did the night of your shooting. Just like you've done in every nightmare since then.*

Sully swallowed hard, his hand sweaty around the gun butt, despite the chill of the night air. He tried to shove the fear aside, the fear that had forced him to resign from the department. You'll freeze. You'll blow it...the internal voice taunted.

As he drew closer to the building, the night he'd been shot flashed in his mind. The dreadful premonition. The telltale metallic click. The deadly inertia that had kept him from moving.

He shook his head, dispelling the haunting images. He was close enough to the shanty now to hear Burt whistling a Grateful Dead song. No other sounds. No little boy cries. No scuffles.

Drawing a deep breath, Sully burst through the door, gun leveled in front of him. Burt Neiman sat on an old mattress, an array of drugs before him. "Hey..." He stumbled to his feet as Sully entered. "Ah, man...don't tell me." He raised his hands over his head. "I'm busted."

Apart from the mattress, decorated with incriminating evidence, the shanty was empty. Hope fled swiftly, leaving Sully desolate. He'd stumbled on what looked to be a drug transaction. "Turn around and put your hands on the wall," he commanded Burt, who complied like one well versed in the routine.

Patting down Burt, Sully found a knife in the

young man's pocket. He threw it across the room. "Turn around, I've got some questions to ask you."

"Aren't you going to read me my rights?" Burt turned and looked at Sully intently. "Hey...I know you. You're the father of that kid. I saw you and your old lady on TV." Burt frowned. "Look, the police already talked to me about that. I don't know nothing about it."

"Maybe your memory is a little faulty. I'm here to help you refresh it." But Sully already knew this was a dead end.

"Hey, man, I'm telling you the truth," Burt said frantically. "I might sell a little dope now and then, but I'd never kidnap no kid. That's low, man."

"Your brother made a lot of threats when he was convicted."

Burt snorted. "My brother also tells me on a regular basis he's gonna kill me. The man is all talk." He eyed Sully's gun, which had never wavered from its target. "I swear, we had nothing to do with your kid."

Sully lowered the gun so that it pointed to Burt's knee. He smiled thinly, knowing his eyes radiated the cold his body had been absorbing since the moment he heard of Eric's disappearance. "Maybe I should shoot you in the leg to see if that helps you tell the truth." He cocked the hammer—a direct threat.

"I swear. I swear I'm telling the truth." Tears filled Burt's eyes, along with abject terror. "Even if you shoot me, I won't be able to tell you anything different."

Sully uncocked the gun and lowered it to his side. "This is your lucky day, Burt. I believe you." Sully started to leave, then turned back. "But if I find out later that you lied to me...you'll never know what hit you."

Sully walked back to his car, disappointment weighing heavily on his shoulders. He was convinced Burt had been telling the truth. Burt Neiman was nothing but a sniveling punk, and Sully doubted that between him and his brother they'd have the brains to pull off a kidnapping and ransom demand.

What now? Sully got into the car and leaned his head against the steering wheel. When he got back to the house, he'd let Donny know about this shanty and the fact that it was probably a popular place for deals to go down.

But what about Eric? What was left for Sully to do? Should he wait until tomorrow? Hope that the kidnapping was for real, that the kidnapper was a man of honor and would be satisfied with the payment of his ransom?

He rubbed his eyes tiredly, his thoughts confused and fragmented by weariness. He couldn't help but feel as if they had missed something...but what?

For years, the newspapers had lauded him as a hero. He'd received dozens of community honors and tributes. But ultimately, in the end, what kind of a hero was he if he couldn't save his own son?

THERESA WOKE UP as Sully eased himself into bed beside her. "Where have you been?" she asked softly. She pushed her hair away from her face. "I woke up a while ago and you were gone."

"It doesn't matter." The dullness in his voice worried her. She couldn't let Sully lose hope. It was important that they believe that Eric would be all right, important that they stay united in that faith.

She leaned over him, stroked his forehead with her fingers. He closed his eyes, as if finding her touch both painful and comforting. She continued to gently rub his forehead until the pattern of his breathing rhythm deepened and she knew he was asleep.

"Don't you give up, Sullivan Mathews," she whispered. "Don't you dare give up on Eric." *Like you did on yourself.*

She got out of bed, troubled by that thought. Was that what had happened? Had Sully given up on himself? What would make him do such a thing? And was it that loss of faith in himself that had made him resign from the force...begin to drink...leave her?

She went into the bathroom and started the water in the tub. Crazy thoughts, that was what they were. Sully had left her because he was so unhappy. He'd drunk to escape from his unhappiness. She was crazy to think it was anything else. She was grasping at straws, trying to turn things back into the way they had once been. But there was no going back, and nothing would ever be the same again.

Easing herself into the hot bath, she thought perhaps she was crazy. Crazy with fear...crazy with worry. It was no wonder she sought to explain Sully's leaving her by placing the blame anywhere but on herself. If it wasn't her that had made him leave...then there was a chance for a reconciliation. And the only reason she was thinking about a reconciliation was that Eric was gone and she was so alone. The thought of a life without Sully...and without Eric...was terrifying.

She leaned her head back against the cool porcelain of the tub. By this time tomorrow night, would Eric be home safe and sound, snug in his bed? Tomorrow night...Christmas Eve.

She caught a sob with the back of her hand against her mouth, knowing that if she allowed one to release itself, others would follow. She didn't want to cry, had already cried too many tears.

She didn't know how long she remained in the tub, but when she finally got out, the water was tepid. In the darkness of the bedroom, while Sully slept, she tugged on a pair of slacks and an oversize sweatshirt, then went out into the kitchen, where Donny half dozed in a chair at the table. He sat up straighter as she entered the room.

"You should go stretch out on the sofa," she said sympathetically. He'd put in a lot of hours over the past two days.

"Nah, I'm all right. I'm going to head home in another hour or so. We'll need to get started early in the morning, preparing for the drop tomorrow afternoon."

Theresa shivered, a phantom cold hand stroking

up her back, as she thought of delivering the ransom money. Her fear was not for herself, but for Eric.

"Did you see the evening paper?" Donny asked.

"No."

He shoved the paper across the table toward her. "You and Sully made the front page."

Theresa sat and looked at the headline. "'Family Prays for Christmas Miracle.'" She laughed without humor. "The press sure knows how to play up a story, don't they." She traced a finger over the photo. She looked like a shell-shock victim, while Sully looked strong and vital.

"He's always been a photogenic cuss," Donny said, as if reading her thoughts.

Theresa smiled. "There was a time when it seemed like Sully's picture was in the paper every other day."

Donny grinned wryly. "Tell me about it. It was sometimes tough working in his shadow."

Theresa looked at him in surprise. She'd never thought about how difficult it might be working as Sully's partner. Sully had been the star of the department, the golden boy of law enforcement. "Sully never cared about his publicity. He just wanted to do his job."

"Yeah, that's what made it okay," Donny agreed. "Sully never let the attention go to his head." He grinned again. "If he had, he would have caught hell from all us guys at the station."

Theresa pushed the paper aside and stood once again, too restless to sit, too tired to think. She walked over to the window and stared out. Ebony night, broken by her own version of a candle in the window...the Christmas lights that would remain burning bright until Eric was returned.

"Are they going to let him go when they get the money?" she asked, still looking into the night.

"I can't answer that," Donny said softly. "I wish I could say an unequivocal yes, but you'd know it was a lie." He was silent for a moment. "We can only hope," he finally added. "I'm letting the feds in on this.... I'll talk to them in the morning and tell them we think we have a potential kidnapping."

Theresa nodded, then frowned as she eyed the dark house next door. "I don't understand why I haven't heard from Rose and Vincent," she said more to herself than to Donny.

"Rose and Vincent?"

She turned away from the window. "My next door neighbors. Rose and Vincent Caltino. I can't figure out why they haven't been over to see me. They adore Eric, and certainly can't have missed the activity going on here."

Donny sat up straighter. "When was the last time you saw them?" He flipped open his notebook.

Theresa stared at him in shock. "Oh, no, surely you don't think..."

"Theresa...when was the last time you saw either of these people?" Donny's voice snapped with a trace of impatience.

Once again Theresa sank down in the chair across from him, this time because she feared her legs would no longer hold her up. "Yesterday." God, had it only been yesterday when she stood at the oven, making cookies for Eric to decorate? It felt like a lifetime ago. "Rose came by yesterday to bring Eric a Christmas present."

"What time did she come by?"

Theresa rubbed her forehead thoughtfully. "Right around time for Eric to come home from school...three-thirty or so." Horror battled with disbelief. "Oh, but Donny, they're a nice older couple. They have no children of their own, so they sort of adopted Eric as an unofficial grandson."

Donny frowned and stood. "I'm going over there and check things out. You wait here." He pulled on his coat and left through the back door.

Theresa moved back to the window and watched as the officer disappeared around the corner of the house. Rose and Vincent? Surely it wasn't possible.

Rose once told you her greatest heartache was in not having children, a little inner voice reminded Theresa. Was it possible Rose and Vincent had loved Eric so much they decided to make him their own? Take him away and keep him until he forgot Theresa's face...her name?

"No." She couldn't believe it. She wouldn't believe it. Rose had a heart of gold, and that heart would never allow her to steal another woman's child. But why hadn't she heard from them?

Minutes ticked by...long, agonizing minutes. Let them be in bed, she prayed. Maybe they'd both come down with the flu...hadn't read the papers...hadn't seen the activity on Theresa's lawn, didn't realize the drama that was being played out.

They were her friends. Since she moved here, they had become like part of her family. She'd trusted them implicitly. Surely there was a logical explanation for them not coming by here, not offering their support, not knowing about Eric's disappearance.

She opened the door when she saw Donny approach. "Nobody is home. The house is dark and there's no car in the garage." He shrugged out of his coat. "Did they mention a trip to you? Perhaps visiting relatives over the holidays?"

Theresa shook her head. "They have no family, and they would have told me if they were leaving."

"I'm going to have a couple of officers see what they can find out about this. How do you spell their last name?"

Theresa spelled the name, fighting against an overwhelming sense of betrayal. As Donny used the phone to call the station, she went back to the window. Where had they gone? "What do we do now?" she asked when Donny had finished his call.

"We wait. DMV will tell us their license-plate numbers, and we'll put out an alert on the car. In the meantime, there's nothing we can do but wait."

"I'm going to lie down," Theresa said, her stomach aching. She left the kitchen, feeling as though her entire world had been turned upside down. She no longer knew who to trust...who to suspect.

In the darkness of the bedroom, she took off her

clothes and pulled on a nightgown. Careful not to disturb Sully, she got into bed next to him.

Despite the fact that she tried to be careful, Sully stirred, although he didn't appear to awaken. In sleep, he reached for her and pulled her into him, spoon-fashion, his arm around her.

In that instant, Theresa knew she was still hopelessly in love with her ex-husband. Instead of bringing her comfort, the knowledge merely deepened the feeling that she was helplessly alone.

Chapter Nine

December 24

The stench of the alley. The long, narrow passage. Fear gripped Sully as he walked between the towering buildings on either side. Paralyzing fear... nauseating terror...accompanied him as he reached the place at the end where Louie stood. A metallic click.

"Help," Louie cried. "Do something."

Sully stood frozen. Frozen with fear.

"For God's sake, man," Louie said, just before the first shot snuffed out his life. As he fell against the trash cans, his face melted, transformed into Eric's features. "Help me, Daddy. Help me...." Eric said, just before he closed his eyes in death.

Sully felt the subsequent bullets ripping into his own body.

He jerked awake with a deep moan. The sheets were hopelessly twisted around him, and he raked his hand across his face, as if to prove to himself he was in bed...not in that godforsaken alley.

"Sully?" Theresa's voice drifted to him from the other side of the bed. "Are you all right?"

"Fine. Just a nightmare." He drew a deep breath, trying to steady the nerves that still jangled inside him, the horror that still coursed through him. "What time is it?"

"Just after seven." She sat up, her hair tousled around her shoulders, her eyes still heavy with sleep.

"Sorry if I woke you."

"You didn't. I've been awake for a while...just lying here resting."

Sully rolled out of bed and padded to the window. Moving the curtains, he peered out. Donny's car was already parked in the driveway, a sleek canary-yellow Corvette. The guys at the station gave him all kinds of static about the flashy car. But Donny had no wife, no children to support, and could indulge his passion for sports cars and expensive clothing.

Press trucks had begun to arrive for another day of news. No sun peeked down from the gray, thick clouds. The sky looked as dismal, as full of tears as Sully felt.

Sully had a bad feeling in his stomach...a feeling not unlike the one he'd had the night when he walked into that alley of death. He rubbed his stomach, vaguely aware of the sounds of Theresa getting dressed. *Maybe it's just left over from the dream,* he told himself. *Maybe it has nothing to do with what's going to happen today.*

Theresa came up behind him, wrapped her arms around his waist and leaned her head against his back. He wanted to turn around and fall into her arms, tell her all the fears he'd hidden since the night of his shooting.

He wanted to confess to her how he feared he'd lost the edge that had made him a good cop, how afraid he was that if he was a cop again and found himself in a threatening situation, he'd freeze. But, of course, he couldn't...wouldn't...talk about his fears to Theresa. He'd never expose his vulnerabilities, his weaknesses, to her.

"I went to talk to Burt Neiman last night." He turned and faced her.

"And?" The hopeful expectation on her face broke his heart.

"And he had nothing to do with Eric's disappearance. I gave him a good incentive to spill his guts, but there was nothing to spill."

"If the Neimans had nothing to do with it, then maybe it really is Rose and Vincent."

Sully frowned. "Rose and Vincent. Aren't they your neighbors? I think Eric has mentioned them before."

She nodded and quickly filled Sully in on what she and Donny had discussed the night before. "Oh, Sully, they were our friends...good friends. If they had anything to do with this, I'll feel so betrayed."

He knew all about how betrayal felt, knew intimately the bad taste it left in your mouth, the sickness that invaded your soul. A sickness that never really healed.

Theresa squared her shoulders, a look of grim determination on her face. "I'd better get out there and talk to Donny, see what he's learned."

Sully nodded. "I'll be out in a few minutes. I want to take a fast shower."

Minutes later, as he stood beneath the shower, Sully once again thought of the betrayal he'd felt after his shooting. He'd been certain that he'd been set up. Although the official ruling was that Sully had been in the wrong place at the wrong time and the target had been the snitch. Sully had believed with every fiber of his being that it was just the opposite. Louie had been in the wrong place at the wrong time, and Sully had been the target.

But when Sully went to the chief with his suspicions, the old man had exploded. "You're accusing your brothers, your fellow officers," he'd ranted. "Think about it, Sully—what possible motivation could those men have to want you dead?"

And now there was another crime with no obvious motivation, for there was no way Sully could believe that Eric's kidnapping was about money.

But to think that the two incidents were related was crazy. Or was it? Two of the officers he'd told he was meeting Louie at the usual place were assigned to Eric's case. Donny and Kip. He ducked his head beneath the water, knowing he was reaching for straws, clutching at fantasies, to find answers.

Donny had been a terrific partner, and they'd shared a friendship in the years they worked together. Kip had become a valuable friend to Sully since the night of the shooting. Both were doing everything in their power to get Eric back.

By the time he got out of the shower, his head was back on straight. Today was the day, hopefully, they'd get some answers. After the drop was made, surely Eric would be released. Please God.

Walking through the living room, he kept his eyes averted from the Christmas tree, with its flickering lights and its yawning emptiness at the top. When he got to the door that led to the kitchen, he paused, his gaze reluctantly going to the tree.

Tonight was Christmas Eve. *Let Eric be here for me to lift up. Let him be here to place the angel where she belongs.* Sully wondered whether God accepted bargaining. *Let him come home, and I'll never drink again. Let him be safe, and I'll be the best damned father in the entire universe. Just give me back my son safe and sound, and I'll do whatever you want me to.*

Tearing his gaze from the tree, Sully entered the kitchen. Half a dozen policemen stood around the table, where Donny had blueprints spread out before him. Sully looked at the prints and realized it was a drawing of the Pineridge shopping mall.

"Sully." Donny nodded a curt hello, then went back to instructing the men.

Sully walked over to where Theresa stood, near the back door, a cup of coffee in her hand. "This all seems so unreal," she said softly.

"They know what they're doing," Sully assured her.

"Okay...we meet in the security office at the mall at one o'clock," Donny finished, then waved his hands to dismiss the men. When all of them had left the kitchen, Donny turned to Sully and Theresa. "I got a court order late last night to check out your neighbors' house. Nobody is home, and it looks like they left in a hurry. Clothes were tossed helter-skelter on the bed, and there were enough missing hangers in the closets for us to surmise that they packed a bag before leaving."

"I can't believe this." Theresa squeezed her eyes tightly closed, and Sully put an arm around her shoulder. She leaned into him for a moment, then straightened once again. "So what now?" she asked, looking at Donny.

"Their license-plate number, along with the make and model of their car, has gone out to every station in four surrounding states. If they made the ransom demand, then they haven't left the city yet. They'll want to get their money before heading out. And if they show up at the mall, we'll get them."

"So, you're sure it's them," Theresa asked dully.

Donny looked at her sympathetically. "No, we aren't sure. But at this point they certainly can't be discounted as suspects." He gestured them into seats at the table.

"There's good news and bad news," he continued as they both sat. "The mall is going to be packed. That's good because it will allow all my undercover men to blend in easily. It's bad because it will make everything more difficult to control."

"What happens after I drop off the money?" Theresa asked.

"Nothing. We monitor the trash can, wait for somebody to retrieve the ransom," Donny explained.

"And once that person is in custody, he'll tell where Eric is, won't he." Theresa's words weren't a question, but rather a statement of belief. She looked at Donny, then at Sully, waiting for confirmation of her statement.

Sully and Donny looked at each other. Both knew these cases didn't always have positive outcomes. The sick dread that had begun when Sully awakened once again filled his chest.

THE MORNING PASSED in a haze for Theresa. The kitchen had the feel of a command post in a war. Plans were drawn and redrawn, strategy weighed and evaluated. Policemen came and went like waves of ants, getting orders, receiving commands, either unable to meet Theresa's gaze or offering pitying glances that made her want to scream.

Robert arrived at ten, bringing with him a briefcase filled with money. Tens and twenties, nonsequentially numbered, the bills filled the case. Donny took the case, then dismissed him with a curt nod of his head.

Robert took Theresa's hand and led her into the living room. "Terri, honey. I know this must be horrid for you." He pulled her into his arms and stroked her hair.

Theresa stood stiffly in his embrace. Although his

arms offered comfort, she found none there. He couldn't know what she was going through, couldn't begin to fathom the utter terror she'd felt for the past two days. Only Sully could now. And only Sully's arms comforted.

Gently but firmly, she pulled away from him. He caught her hands and squeezed them tight. "I know you don't see it now, but going through this is just going to make us closer, bond us through trauma. Adversity like this always brings people together."

"Robert." She freed her hands from his and took a step back. "I really appreciate your help with the money. And I consider you a dear friend, but our relationship isn't going any further."

He frowned and reached for her again, but she sidestepped his advance. "You're upset...not thinking clearly. Once Eric is home safe and sound, we'll talk again."

Theresa only nodded, too overwhelmed with thoughts of the ransom-money delivery to argue with Robert about a relationship that didn't exist...would never exist.

"You sure you don't want me to stick around here?" he asked as she led him toward the front door.

"No. Officer Holbrook doesn't want anyone here." It was a lie, but she considered it a forgivable one. She didn't want Robert here. She needed to be focused solely on Eric and the delivery of the ransom-demand money in a couple of hours.

"I'll call you later," Robert said at the door.

"I'll call you," she countered.

He kissed her on the cheek, then left. She watched him as he walked to his car, fighting the impulse to swipe at the place where he'd kissed.

She'd told him the truth. She was grateful that he'd been able to make getting the ransom money together effortless. She shook her head softly, wondering how in the world he thought this kind of adversity could ever unite him and her together in any kind of relationship.

Robert's hope of some sort of love match coming from all this was as crazy as the crank caller telling her to bury a black cat's whiskers in her backyard.

"Theresa?" Sully stepped into the living room. "We need you in here. We're going over everything one last time before leaving for the mall."

Shoving aside thoughts of Robert, Theresa followed Sully back into the kitchen.

By one o'clock that afternoon, they were all situated in the security office at the Pineridge mall, waiting for two o'clock, when Theresa would make the drop.

The office was small but technologically superb, with a bank of video displays showing various areas of the mall. Cameras could be moved with a simple switch here in the control area. Donny instructed the security cop in charge of the cameras where to point each one to get optimal panoramic views of the area surrounding the trash can in front of the Dillards store.

Theresa stared at the bank of video displays, fighting a sense of panic. People mobbed the mall, all seeking the last of the presents to be opened the next morning. A frantic pace moved them along, children whining and tempers flaring as mothers and fathers sought to fulfill dreams without breaking their budgets.

She studied each screen, seeking the face she loved...Eric's face...amid the crowd. Even though she knew it wouldn't be there, she couldn't help but look...hope...pray.

"Nervous?" Sully moved over to stand next to her.

"No... Yes." She flashed him a tight smile. "Actually, I'm terrified. Not for me," she hurriedly added, her gaze going back to the monitors. "I'm terrified something might go wrong, the kidnapper will realize I've come with the police. I'll drop the bag and the money will fly in the air. I'm terrified that when Christmas morning comes, our tree will still not have its angel...and I still won't have my son."

He pulled her hard against his chest. "I'm terrified, too," he breathed into her hair.

She looked up at him in surprise. "Sullivan Mathews scared? I didn't think you ever felt fear."

His eyes darkened. "You have no idea." The words seemed to seep out of him, as if escaping some enormous pressure.

Theresa searched his face, surprised both by his uncharacteristic admission of fear and by the vulnerability his features radiated. During all the dangerous cases he worked when they were together, she'd never seen a flicker of fear in his eyes. And never had she loved him more than she did at this moment, with her own fear reflecting in his eyes.

"Okay...let's go through this one last time." Donny's voice interrupted Theresa's thoughts, pulling them back to the matter at hand. "Now, when you leave this office you go down the corridor and turn left. Take the escalator down to the lower level and stay to the right. Keep to the right side until you reach the trash can, then turn and come back exactly the same way."

Donny shoved the briefcase of money toward Sully, along with a paper bag. "Want to transfer that money to the bag?" Sully nodded and got to work.

Donny looked at Theresa once again. "Don't stop to talk to anyone, no matter who it might be. We have to assume you'll be watched, and you don't want to do anything that might be construed as threatening to the kidnapper."

With each moment that ticked by, with every instruction given to her, Theresa's heart quickened with fear. So many details...so much room for error. And her little boy's life hanging in the balance.

At ten minutes to two, Donny handed her the paper bag with the money inside. "We'll be watching you every step of the way," he assured her.

However, it wasn't Donny's words that assured her, it was the look in Sully's eyes that eased her trembling, imbued her with strength. "It's going to be fine," he said softly, then leaned down and kissed her.

With the imprint of his lips still warming her own, Theresa stepped out of the security office and into the chaos of the mall.

As she walked toward the escalator, her senses seemed unnaturally heightened. The ringing of a bell by a pseudo-Santa gathering spare change for charity jangled discordantly with the soft Christmas carol wafting through the air. The scents of bayberry and peppermint battled with heavy perfumes and the smell of flavored popcorn, causing Theresa's stomach to roll in protest.

She stared at the men who passed her. The man with the funny winter hat...did he have Eric? The man in the three-piece suit...was he the kidnapper?

She held the sack of money against her heart as she stepped onto the escalator. She scanned the faces of the shoppers who came into view as the moving stairs took her to the lower level of shops. Were Rose and Vincent here...waiting for her to drop off the money? Or was a stranger watching her...trading money for her heart?

As she approached the Dillards store, she recognized Kip, a hat pulled low on his forehead as he sat at a bench nearby. He had a newspaper in one hand, a hot dog in the other. He didn't look up as she walked past him, but she had a feeling that, despite his nonchalant air, he missed nothing that was happening around them.

When she reached the trash can, she dropped the bag inside, turned and headed back the way she had come. Instantly, all her energy, all her strength, seemed to disappear. She walked back to the security office on legs that trembled. The tension, the worry...the gnawing emptiness...were suddenly overwhelming as she prayed that this day would end with her son back in her arms.

Tears blurred her vision and streaked down her cheeks. It was over. She had done what she needed to do. Now she could only pray the kidnapper would keep his word.

Sully met her at the office door, as if he'd known how great her need to be held would be. And that was what he did. Held her. While Donny studied the monitors, while dozens of officers kept their attention focused on a trash can, while agonizing minutes passed...Sully held tight to Theresa.

Someplace beyond the horror, in spite of the anguish over Eric, Theresa realized that she and Sully still had unfinished business. There was still a bond of love between them, a strong, shining strand that the divorce hadn't been able to snap. She had never understood the reasons why Sully left her, had assumed and guessed, but had never really known.

With his arms tight around her, feeling his love suffusing her, she knew that before this was all over she'd demand some answers from him. And this time she wouldn't let him walk away until she had the answers.

"Sully, you and Theresa need to go back to her place. I'll send Kip with you," Donny instructed.

Theresa pulled away from Sully's arms. "Why? I

want to stay here. I want to be here when they let Eric go.''

"That might not happen here," Sully said, his voice gentle, as if he were aware of the tenuous control she was fighting desperately to maintain.

"Just because they had you drop the money here doesn't mean this is where they'll release Eric," Donny explained, his gaze not wavering from the monitor in front of him. "They might contact you by phone, tell you where Eric has been released."

"Come on, I'll drive you two home," Kip said.

AS THEY DROVE toward Theresa's house, Sully recognized the shaky control his ex-wife fought to maintain within herself. She clutched his hand, as if lost, as if he were the anchor that kept her moored to sanity. He'd never seen her so needy, so weak. He wanted to wrap his arms around her and hold her forever, keep the world with its monsters at bay. But he couldn't. The monster had already entered their life and stolen their son.

He knew she'd believed that the moment she dropped the money into the trash can, Eric would miraculously appear, like a rabbit pulled from a magician's hat.

Nobody spoke on the way home. There were no words left for any of them. When they reached the house, the press stood waiting, a vocal single entity with dozens of talking heads.

"Where'd you go?"

"Have you heard from Eric?"

"What's happened in the past several hours?"

Questions pelted them as they walked up the sidewalk and into the house. Fifteen messages awaited them on the answering machine. Two crank calls, three reporters, the rest friends and neighbors offering condolences and help. As they listened to each one, Sully saw the hope slowly ebb from Theresa's eyes.

"What if they never let him go?" she said. She stared at Sully with dull, lifeless eyes. "Robert said this kind of thing brings people closer, makes them stronger. But it doesn't. It destroys them." She pressed a hand against her mouth as tears silently oozed from her eyes.

Her weakness made Sully reach inside himself to find his strength. "Theresa, you can't give up hope now. Eric could be home at any moment."

"And he could be...dead." The word they'd all danced around, the possibility they'd refused to acknowledge, fell from her lips on a moan.

"No!" Sully's protest exploded from him, making Theresa jump. He grabbed her hands and held them against his heart. "It's just like you told me before. I still feel him, here in my heart. I know he's alive." Sully's voice rang with his conviction and, to his relief, he saw the dark emptiness of her eyes filling with a spark of renewed life...returned faith.

"Oh, Sully. How did we lose each other?" Her eyes pierced his, as if she were attempting to see the secrets in his soul. Secrets he couldn't share with her.

"Nothing has been right since you left. I miss you. I want you back in my life, back in our life."

The unexpected words were like gunshots delivering bullets into his flesh. Each one sharp, causing piercing pain. He yearned to give in to the images her words produced...the sweet thought of a future filled with Theresa and Eric. He longed for that future filled with laughter and love.

But it was a false image, for he could never be the man she needed, would never again be the man he wanted himself to be.

"Theresa, we're both under a lot of stress." He stepped away from her, needing some distance. If he'd ever been strong in his life, he needed to be strong now. But he couldn't be with the scent of her perfume filling his head, the warmth of her body heat so achingly close.

He walked across the room, then turned to face her once again. "Our world has been turned upside down. You're reaching out to me right now because of everything that's going on. We can't make decisions, changes, in the midst of all this turmoil."

She stared at him for another long moment, the flicker of life in her eyes intensified with a spark of something akin to anger. It sparkled and rippled, then faded away. "You're right, Sully. Now isn't the time to make any decisions. But sooner or later, I want you to tell me all the things you didn't tell me about the night you were shot. Sooner or later, you're going to have to explain to me how a bullet in your chest so effectively killed our marriage.'' Without waiting for his reply, she turned and left the kitchen.

Sully closed his eyes and drew a deep, weary breath. They'd never talked about that night.

Oh, he'd told her the bare facts after he came out of surgery. She'd sat with him day after day during his recuperation, but he'd never told her of his suspicions. He'd never talked to her about his fears. He hadn't explained to her that on that night, the man she loved had died, and a weak, ineffectual coward had taken his place.

Chapter Ten

The evening hours seemed to last forever. Sully and Theresa took turns pacing the living room, while Kip sat at the kitchen table, eating the pizza he'd had delivered around six o'clock.

Kip maintained radio contact with the officers at the mall, who so far had nothing to report. Nobody suspicious had gone near the trash can, and they intended to remain monitoring until the mall closed at eleven that night. Then, if the money hadn't been picked up, the situation would have to be reassessed.

Sully wandered the house, roaming like a burglar casing the place. Tension knotted the muscles in his neck, made sitting still absolutely impossible.

He would have liked to stay at the mall, watch that trash can until the perpetrator sidled up to it to grab his money. He'd like to wrap his fingers around the guilty party's neck…shake him until they got some answers. But he knew Donny had been right to send them home. Home, where a call might come in, telling them Eric was at the corner of Tenth Street and Oak…or at a grocery store on Main Street.

But the calls that occasionally interrupted the quiet continued to be useless...neighbors and acquaintances, reporters and media, people offering help or wanting a story.

Sully found himself in Eric's bedroom, breathing in the scent of boyhood. There was so many things he hadn't experienced yet with Eric. So many unfulfilled promises and yet-to-be-reached dreams.

He'd promised the boy a fishing trip this summer, looked forward to helping him work on his knuckleball. Dammit, he'd had plans...dreams for Eric...and the thought that those dreams might not ever be fulfilled broke his heart.

"Sully?" Theresa appeared in the doorway. "Are you okay?"

"Yeah, I thought maybe the hamster might need some food," he said, improvising.

She nodded. "Eric will be mad if he gets home and we haven't taken care of Petey."

Sully poured some fresh pellets of food into the dish in the hamster cage. Petey stuck his little pink nose out of the cedar shavings, then retreated once again into sleep.

"Come out here and sit with me," Theresa said.

They went back into the living room, where Montana immediately curled up on the sofa next to Theresa. She patted the dog on the head. "He acts like he's been here forever."

"I'm sorry I didn't check it out with you before getting him," Sully said as he eased down in the chair next the fireplace. "To be honest, I didn't know

I was going to get him until the day I saw him in the pet shop. He looked at me with those big brown eyes, and I was lost. Then, when the store owner told me his name, I knew this mutt was destined to belong to Eric.''

Theresa smiled and stroked the dog's rich coat. ''It's okay. Eric will be wild for him.'' Her gaze remained fixed on Sully. ''You look good, Sully. You've lost some weight, but it becomes you.''

''Getting off the booze didn't hurt.''

''I'm so proud of you, Sully. I know how difficult it is to put something like that behind you.''

He averted his gaze from hers. He didn't want her pride. If he was truly a good man, he'd never have fallen into the trap of alcohol in the first place. ''Yeah, well, I thought about how I felt about my father, and I never wanted Eric to feel that way about me.'' He knew he didn't have to say anything further.

Theresa knew all about his father's alcoholism, the disease having finally killed him when Sully was twenty-four. Theresa knew that Sully had loved his father, but also that his love had been tempered with resentment and anger that sometimes flirted with actual hate.

''Eric could never feel differently about you than he does,'' Theresa said gently. ''He loves you, Sully. Next to Joe Montana, you're his hero.''

Sully laughed. ''Yeah, I never could quite compete with old Joe.'' He sobered. ''Anyway, I like my life now that I'm sober. It works for me.''

He saw the hurt that darkened Theresa's eyes at his words, but knew it was important she believe his words. He had to make sure she entertained no hopes for a reconciliation.

It had nearly undone him when she told him she still loved him, wanted them back together as a family. But he knew her words of love had probably come from the stress of the situation, their bond through Eric.

All he had to do was look around to see that she'd done fine without him. She'd provided Eric with a good home, one that radiated love and warmth and happiness. He didn't belong here, and he wasn't about to be seduced by emotion into the position where she would see the damage inside him, the crippling fear that left him less than a whole man.

She deserved better. A man like Robert Cassino, with his smooth good looks and adoring smile. Sully's stomach clenched at thoughts of the banker. "How long have you been dating Robert?"

She frowned. "We aren't really dating, so to speak. We've gone to dinner together half a dozen times. The three of us went to the movies twice. It's really not a big deal."

Sully remembered the way Robert had looked at Theresa. It might not be a big deal to her, but it was definitely a big deal to Robert. He fancied himself in love with Theresa.

"And what was it he said to you? Something about this adversity bringing you closer together?"

She nodded, her hair falling over her shoulder in

a dark spill. Sully clenched his hands, fighting the impulse to wrap his hands in its softness, breathe deeply of its fragrance. He'd always loved her hair. "He hoped going through this ordeal would bring us closer together. Fat chance," she said derisively. "What this ordeal has done is make me realize I don't want to see him anymore. He's not the man I want in my life or Eric's life."

Sully rubbed his forehead, crazy thoughts taking form in his brain. Was it possible? It seemed too ridiculous to even consider...and yet... "You don't suppose it's possible that Robert engineered this whole kidnapping?"

Theresa stared at him as if he'd lost his mind. And perhaps he had. "Oh, Sully...why would he do something like that?"

"I don't know...some crazy scheme to bring you and him closer together?" The longer he thought about it, the less crazy it seemed. A long shot, yes. But long shots were all they had in their possession. "He provides the ransom money and becomes a hero in your eyes."

"And he doesn't have to worry about losing the ransom money because he intends to retrieve it from the trash can." Theresa followed his thought process. "It sounds so crazy...and yet it makes a crazy kind of sense."

"I'm going to talk to Kip, see if he can get some men to check it out."

"WHY HASN'T ANYONE tried to pick up the money? Why haven't we heard anything about Eric?" Theresa felt as if she'd shatter into a hundred pieces if they didn't hear anything soon.

Christmas Eve. She and Sully should be whispering secrets, wrapping last-minute presents and glorying in the season of love and peace. Instead, Eric was missing and Sully had retreated into a shell of silence.

She flopped onto the sofa and stared at him with a touch of resentment. He'd made her angry earlier, when he dismissed her plea that they get back together so easily. And again when he stressed that he was happy with his life now...as if he'd been so unhappy with his life with her.

But with the passing of hours, she'd realized he was probably right. She was overwrought, under too much stress to make decisions that would affect her future.

And yet her head couldn't deny what her heart knew. She loved Sully, would probably always love him. But even though the tragedy of Eric's disappearance had brought them momentarily together, closer than they had been since their divorce, there would be no happily-ever-after for them.

She'd bared her heart to Sully, told him her desire that they be together again. She hadn't missed the fear her words provoked in his eyes. She'd known then that hers were the dreams of a fool. She was part of Sully's past, and he had no intention of repeating his mistakes.

Sully sat down next to her, offering her a small smile of truce, one that only made her love him more.

"This waiting is horrid," she said, breaking the silence that had filled the room.

"I know. Theresa..." He turned and looked at her, as if he'd made a decision, come to a conclusion. "About the night I got shot." He leaned back and closed his eyes for a moment. When he looked at her once again, a steady resolve darkened his eyes. "We never talked about it.... I never told you exactly what happened that night."

"Talk to me now, Sully," she prompted.

He raked a hand over his face. "I don't even know where to begin...."

"Just talk," Theresa replied, wanting him to fill the silence, a silence that had lingered far too long between the two of them.

"Donny and I had cultivated a number of street snitches, punks who worked both sides of the law. Louie was one of Donny's punks, a paranoid loser who occasionally came up with useful information about cases we were working." He stood, obviously needing movement to keep the words flowing.

"On this particular night, Louie called and said he had some big information. About an hour before he called, Donny had left sick. I knew better than to go alone, but hell, I was the great Sullivan Mathews...crime-stopper extraordinaire. I figured I could handle one punk snitch." His face twisted with a bitterness that tore into her heart.

"Sully, you can't blame yourself. You'd met snitches alone before," she said softly.

He nodded. "You're right." He sank down in the chair across from her, his eyes as dark and cold as the night falling outside the window. "But I knew this time was different the moment I got out of my car."

"What? What made this time different?" Theresa asked as she leaned forward. The ache of waiting, the emptiness of Eric's absence, momentarily fell aside as Theresa delved into the unknown events that she suspected caused Sully's nightmares.

Sully frowned, the lines across his forehead deepening. "I'm not sure.... Something...something made me wary, apprehensive, but...but..." He sighed in frustration. "The memory is just out of my reach."

"Leave it for now.... It will come to you," Theresa said, not wanting him to stop talking, hoping for some sort of answer that would explain the wreck they had made of their life together. "What happened in that alley, Sully? I know Louie was killed, and you were shot, but something happened to you that you never told me. You changed that night, Sully...and whatever it was, it was more than the bullet that hit your body."

He leaned back in the chair, a gray pallor sweeping over his skin as he dived into the landscape of his nightmares. "You know what the official story is...that whoever Louie was about to rat on shut him up. I just got in the way, was a misfortunate bystander."

"Okay...that's the official version. Now, what's your version?" She could see the battle taking place inside him, the need to talk battling the need to keep whatever it was within.

"I promised myself I wouldn't talk about it anymore. The chief thought I was crazy when I told him."

"Tell me, Sully. I won't think you're crazy."

He cast her a half smile...an echo of the Sully she'd once known. "You haven't heard me yet." The smile faded, replaced by torment. "I think I was set up."

"Set up?" Theresa frowned in confusion. "By whom?"

"By one of my fellow officers."

She met his statement with stunned silence. He forced another smile. "Crazy, huh?"

"Not crazy," she countered. She knew Sully well enough to know he wouldn't jump to such a conclusion without reason. She also knew that if he believed such a betrayal had taken place, it would explain his drinking and his resignation from the department. Sully had believed in the brotherhood of the blue...and if he believed one of his brothers had set him up for murder, then his sacred trust had been corrupted, and that was enough to break a man.

She left the sofa and went to his side, sitting on the floor at his feet. "Tell me why you think this, Sully. You must have reasons."

He smiled, and it was once again a reflection of the bitterness that ate at him inside. "That's the problem—there's nothing specific I can put my finger on as proof." He raked a hand through his hair, a familiar gesture Theresa recognized as intense frustration. "I don't know...maybe when the surgeons cut that bullet out, they took my sense with it."

"Your instincts have always been terrific, Sullivan, don't discount them now."

This time his smile was genuine, almost grateful, as he took her hand in his. "I've thought and thought about that night. What keeps playing in my mind is that if the shooter was after Louie, he got him. A perfect shot to the forehead. Why take the risk of shooting me, unless I was the primary target?"

"Maybe the shooter just went crazy?" Theresa was trying to play the devil's advocate.

"Maybe," he replied, but she heard the doubt in his voice. "But most criminals would rather do anything than kill a cop and bring down the wrath of the whole department on their heads. Besides, it's more than that." He frowned again, released her hand and rubbed his forehead. "It's a gut feeling, one with no rhyme or reason...just there."

"Who knew when and where you were meeting this Louie?" she asked, crossing her arms and leaning on his knee.

"Five men knew. The chief, Barry Walker, Tony Marcias, Kip and Donny." Again his hand raked through his hair. "Sometimes I'm sure I've lost my mind, and other times I know somebody I trusted tried to kill me."

"Sully, why didn't you tell me this before? Why have you carried this burden alone for all this time?" It hurt, that all the days and nights she sat with him in the hospital, at a time she thought their marriage was strong enough to withstand the blow, he'd kept this from her, refused to share what was in his heart. It made her realize that the marriage she'd thought so strong, so good, had only been an illusion, a dream, without substance.

Cold winds of despair swept through her as the ache of the unknown where Eric was concerned was coupled with this new emptiness.

"Sorry to interrupt," Kip said as he entered the living room from the kitchen. "Just thought you might want to know they found your neighbors at the Ramada Inn in St. Louis."

Theresa stood, heart banging against her ribs. "Eric?" she asked breathlessly.

Kip shook his head. "No sign of him, and no indication that your neighbors had anything to do with his disappearance."

"What are they doing in St. Louis?" Sully asked, also rising from his seat.

"According to the officer who interviewed them, the husband decided to surprise the wife with an anniversary trip."

Theresa closed her eyes, remembering Rose mentioning Vincent's secretiveness. She'd forgotten all about their approaching anniversary on the twenty-eighth of the month. Relief flooded through her as she realized that the couple she'd come to love hadn't betrayed her love and trust.

The relief was short-lived, quickly swallowed by a despair so deep, so dark, it nearly stole her breath away. "Why haven't we heard anything?" she asked Sully. "For God's sakes, why haven't they let him go?"

She felt her control slipping, sliding out of her grasp, and she welcomed the flirtation with insanity. Picking up a glass candlestick, she threw it against the fireplace. It shattered into a thousand pieces, and she shattered with it. "We paid them...we gave them the money...so where is Eric? Why haven't they released him? Where is our son?"

Sully grabbed her and pulled her roughly against his chest, holding her tight, as if trying to keep her together. Theresa had always prided herself on being strong, keeping control. Those were qualities that had gotten her through a difficult childhood, characteristics that made her a damn good prosecutor. But at the moment, she was simply a woman whose heart was breaking, a mother who needed her child.

"Shh..." Sully consoled her as Kip disappeared back into the kitchen. He patted her back, then caressed her hair as she wept into the front of his shirt, releasing pent-up tension along with her tears.

She cried for the marriage that would never be fixed. She mourned Sully's shattered innocence on the night he'd been shot, and she cried for the little boy lost to them both.

"We're going to get him back, Theresa." Sully's voice rang with strength, as if, when it left her, he'd breathed it in.

She nodded, wanting to believe him, needing to believe. She stood another minute in his embrace, then moved away, knowing she had to stop depending on Sully.

He had his own demons to slay, and he'd made it clear that he didn't want, or need, her help. She had to put any thoughts of a reconciliation behind her, and she had to regain her courage, her fortitude...for Eric.

Looking at her watch, she realized it was almost nine o'clock. As Sully had told her about the night of his shooting, the evening hours had slipped away.

Nine o'clock. Christmas Eve. If Eric was here, they'd be giggling in the kitchen, filling a plate of cookies for Santa. They had a litany of rituals that had become Christmas traditions through the years.

And by abandoning those rituals on this night, she feared, she'd be abandoning Eric. With that thought in mind, she went into the kitchen.

Kip looked up in surprise as she went to the refrigerator and pulled out a gallon of milk, then got the cocoa and sugar from the cabinet. As she mixed the ingredients in a saucepan, Sully came into the kitchen.

He seemed to know exactly what she was doing. As she warmed the cocoa mixture, he opened cabinets until he found the one with the cookies.

They worked separately, but in tune, Sully fixing

both a platter and a saucer of cookies, while Theresa poured three cups of hot cocoa and a glass of milk.

"Come and have a cup of cocoa with us, Kip," she said to the officer, who was missing Christmas Eve with his family to do his job.

"Sure. That would be nice," Kip agreed as he stood.

Theresa carried a tray of drinks, Sully took the cookies, and Kip followed as they went into the living room. As Theresa handed Kip a mug of the steaming drink, Sully turned the gas on in the fireplace, instantly producing cheerful flames. Montana curled up on the rug in front of the fireplace, as if he, too, were suffering from the same bone-chilling cold that ached inside Theresa.

Under normal circumstances, this time would be filled with Eric's eager chatter, the excitement of a child awaiting the arrival of Santa. But these were not normal circumstances, and the silence of the three adults filled the room more loudly than any child's laughter could have.

When Theresa could stand the hush no longer, she picked up the book they always read together on Christmas Eve. As Sully and Kip sipped their hot cocoa, with the cookies and milk in their appropriate place on the fireplace hearth, Theresa opened the book. "'Twas the night before Christmas..." she began.

ERIC'S FINGERS ACHED from the day's work. He'd spent all the daylight hours pulling, tugging and prying at the nails that held the boards in place over the small window. He'd managed to completely get the lowest board off. But the space was still too small for him to wiggle through. When he finished working for the day, he'd carefully leaned the loose board back into place, not wanting the masked man to know what he'd accomplished.

Night had once again come, and he could hear a cold wind whistling around the window. He sat on the mattress, huddled for warmth, hands jammed into his pockets.

He'd eaten the last of the food, and that worried him. Would the masked man come back? Bring him more food? Although his belly was full at the moment, he didn't want to think about having no food. It scared him.

He knew it was Christmas Eve, and he thought of the cookies his mom had bought especially for Santa. Chocolate with double fudge. They were Eric's favorite, so he knew Santa would like them, too. He hoped his mom remembered to put them out even though Eric wasn't home to remind her.

Christmas Eve. He closed his eyes and imagined the Christmas tree, decorated with lights and ornaments and tinsel. The vision made him smile.

Eric had always loved Christmas Eve almost as much as Christmas morning. Every Christmas Eve, his mom made hot cocoa, and they'd all sit around the tree and talk and laugh. Eric loved to hear his dad laugh. It made him all warm and tickly inside.

Funny. He wasn't so scared of the dark tonight.

After two nights in the total darkness, he'd realized there were no monsters in the cellar. And the dark made it easier for him to paint pictures in his mind. Pictures that kept him warm in spite of the cold. Pictures that made the darkness of the room fill with light.

He knew his mom and dad were probably together, worried about him. He liked thinking of them together. He hadn't understood that divorce stuff. He'd told his mom that the thing he wanted most for Christmas was for them to all live together, be a family again. But she'd told him that was a wish Santa couldn't give him. Still, the idea that they were probably together now made him happy, even though he wasn't there with them.

He closed his eyes, feeling the burn of tears. He didn't want to cry. Crying was for babies. But he wished he was home. Except he had a feeling that was another wish that was beyond Santa's control.

Once again he focused on painting the Christmas tree in his mind. He could perfectly imagine the living room, with a cheerful fire in the fireplace, carols playing on the stereo, and the tree shining in the corner. He could almost taste the sweet warmth of hot cocoa sliding down his throat, smell the freshness of pine needles. Before his mother tucked him in bed, she would read out loud.

Eric frowned, trying to remember what it was she read every Christmas Eve. Something about kerchiefs and caps and sashes. Panic swelled inside him as he searched his mind, trying to remember the words that last year he'd nearly known by heart.

It scared him that he didn't remember. What if he stayed down in this cellar so long he forgot what his mom and dad looked like? Forgot his own name?

He had to remember. He had to. And then, suddenly, thankfully, the words came. Relief flooded through him. "'Twas the night before Christmas..." he began, his little voice filling the darkness with hope.

Chapter Eleven

"How could you do this to me?" Robert's voice swelled in Theresa's ear.

She gripped the phone more tightly. "It's nothing personal, Robert. The police are checking out everyone close to me."

"Yeah, but it was so humiliating. I open my door and two cops are standing there on the porch. They also told me that a couple of men were speaking to my secretary and the president of the bank. Something like this could ruin me. My God, Theresa, what were you thinking of?"

"I was thinking of my son," she snapped, then bit back a sigh. Moments earlier, they had gotten word that Robert had an airtight alibi for the day of Eric's disappearance. He'd been at the bank all day, then gone to dinner with a group of friends. "Robert, I'm sorry you were embarrassed, but the police have to do their job." Dear God, her son had been missing for two nights and three days, and this man was complaining to her about a little embarrassment. "Look, I can't tie up this line. I'll talk to you later." She slammed down the phone, suddenly realizing what it was she hadn't liked about Robert. His utter self-involvement. Robert saw the world only as it related to him. Self-important, self-indulgent...Robert was all of those things and more.

"Sometimes crises bring out the worst in people," Kip said softly.

She looked at him and forced a smile. "And sometimes crises make you see the worst that's always been there."

"You and Sully are holding up well," he observed.

"Sully is strong. He gives me my strength."

Kip studied her face for a long moment. "Maybe you need to remind him of that once in a while." Kip bit his lip, as if he were sorry he'd said anything.

"What do you mean?" Theresa looked at the man who probably knew Sully better than anyone at the moment. "You can't just throw out a statement like that without doing a little explaining."

Kip worried a hand through his graying hair. "Sully is battling a lot of internal demons right now. He has been since the night of his shooting. His biggest demon is fear."

"Fear?" She looked at Kip curiously. Sully had alluded to feelings of fear before, but she'd dismissed his words. She looked toward the back door, where Sully had disappeared a little while ago, telling her he needed to walk off some tension. "Fear of what? I've never known Sully to be afraid of anything or anyone."

"Sully believes he's lost his edge, is missing the instincts that made him a good cop."

"Weren't you there that night...when Sully got hurt? I seem to remember you were one of the first men on the scene."

Kip nodded. "I was in my patrol car when the call came in of an officer down." Kip's eyes darkened at the memory. "God, what a scene. Garbage rotting...the night hotter than hell...Louie dead and Sully as near death as a man can get. He was unconscious when I got there. I took off my shirt and pressed it into the wound on his chest, and in the moments before the ambulance arrived, he regained consciousness."

Theresa closed her eyes, grateful she hadn't seen the man she loved lying near death in a stinking alley. Her first view of Sully after the incident had been of him in a sterile hospital bed, surrounded by life-giving machines. She looked at Kip once again. "Did he say anything?"

"Yeah, he told me to tell you and Eric that he loved you." Kip smiled. "I guess he thought he wouldn't get a chance to tell you that himself."

Emotion welled in Theresa's chest. He hadn't. After that night, he'd never spoken of love. Instead, he'd crawled into a shell, retreating from everything and everyone.

"He also told me he froze."

Theresa frowned. "Froze?"

Kip nodded. "Apparently he heard the click of the shooter's gun being cocked, but he froze. That's what eats at him now...the fear that if he's in a deadly situation again, he'll freeze and somebody will get hurt. That's why he started drinking...to stop the fear."

Theresa's head reeled with all the information Kip had just given her. Why hadn't Sully told her any of this? He hadn't started drinking because he was unhappy in the marriage. It had been an effort to quiet his fears.

She got up from the table and poured herself a cup of coffee, her mind working to assess this information, fit it into a proper place. But there seemed no proper place to put it.

It hurt her that Sully hadn't felt close enough to her to bare his soul, that it had taken a fellow officer to tell her what her husband was feeling.

Sully walked in the back door, bringing with him a burst of arctic air. "I think the weather forecasters are finally going to get it right. It definitely feels like snow," he said as he peeled off his coat and threw it across the back of one of the kitchen chairs. He looked at Kip, then at Theresa. "Did I miss anything while I was gone?"

"No. Nothing has changed," Theresa replied briskly, averting her gaze from him. "You want coffee?"

"Sounds good." He took the cup she offered gratefully, then looked at his watch. "We should be hearing something from Donny in a few minutes. It's almost eleven, and the mall will be closing."

Theresa sank back down at the table. "Surely if

the police had seen anyone near the trash bin, they would have called us by now, arrested somebody." She cupped her hands around the warmth of her cup. "Why would a kidnapper tell us to put the money in a trash bin, then not retrieve it? It doesn't make sense."

"These things never make sense."

Senseless tragedy. How often had Theresa seen those words used in a newspaper report about a particular crime? A hundred? A thousand? And now those same words characterized her son's disappearance.

Some parents never found out what happened to their abducted children. Theresa tried to imagine a lifetime of questions...of wondering and waiting. She couldn't imagine it. After three days, she felt the rope of her sanity stretched taut. Eventually, it would snap.

"Theresa, we're going to find him," Sully said, as if he'd read the horrible thoughts filtering through her mind.

"You promise?"

His eyes bored into hers, fiery with intent, yet darkened with the kind of emptiness she felt deep within her. "I promise."

It was almost midnight when Donny and several other officers returned to the house. Theresa could tell in a moment of looking at their faces that they had nothing to tell her, no hope to offer her.

"We waited until the mall was empty, then I went down to the trash can," Donny explained as he took the cup of coffee Theresa offered him. "The money was gone."

Theresa stared at him blankly. "What do you mean...it was gone?" Sully cursed soundly and slammed his hands down on the table.

"How in the hell is that possible?" he asked. "Didn't anyone see anybody go near that can? How did the perp manage to get the money without anyone seeing him?"

"I don't know. I can't explain it," Donny snapped, obviously frustrated by this new turn of events. "I had half a dozen men doing nothing but watching that trash. We never saw anyone suspicious-looking approach it."

"But you saw somebody." Sully stared at the three officers, his face flushed with anger.

"Kids," one of the other men replied after a moment's hesitation.

"What kids?" Theresa asked as she placed a placating hand on Sully's arm.

"There was a point this evening when about five kids were hanging out close to the trash can. You know, wrestling with each other and horsing around," Donny said. "The only thing we can figure, the perp paid off one of the kids to retrieve the paper sack from the trash. With all the other kids around, we never saw it happen."

Sully cursed again. "Dammit, I should have stayed at the mall."

"What could you have done that we didn't do?" Donny retorted.

All the anger seemed to whoosh out of Sully. "I don't know."

"I'm sorry, Sully. We didn't think those kids posed a threat. They weren't even teenagers, they were younger. Who'd have thought..." Donny's voice trailed off. He heaved a deep sigh and drained his coffee. "We're going to pack it in for the night. There's nothing more that can be done here for now."

Within minutes, all the men had gone home. Home to their families, home to put together toys for the morning, to wrap last-minute presents, home to their warm houses, where their own children slept safe and sound.

Theresa stood at the front door, watching as their cars' taillights disappeared into the darkness of night. With them went the last of her hope.

She leaned weakly against the storm door, the pane of glass achingly cold against the heat of her forehead.

She didn't move until Sully gently took her arm and moved her away so that he could close the front door. When she looked at him, she saw the shine of tears on his cheeks, knew he felt the same black despair she did.

She moved into his arms and kissed him, unsure whether she tasted the salt of his tears or her own. They didn't speak. Their pain was beyond words, their need to be in each other's arms too enormous to deny.

His mouth tasted of anguish, the same as her own.

Tears were inadequate to express the emotions roiling inside her. She only knew she wanted to be held by Sully, escape into him.

Where before their kisses had been filled with pent-up passion, the ones they shared now were filled with the unfulfilled hopes and dreams for the little boy they had created together.

As if in silent agreement, they moved to the thick rug in front of the fireplace and silently shed their clothes. Theresa knew Sully had the same need she did...the need to be held, the need for them to love each other for this moment in time. She needed to get lost in a world without thought, and knew he felt the same way. Their need wasn't physical, but rather spiritual.

Theresa turned off the lights, leaving the room illuminated only by the flames in the fireplace and the Christmas lights flashing and chasing one another amid the tree boughs.

As she joined Sully on the rug, for a long moment they merely gazed at each other. His face was a study in contrasts, each feature intensified by the play of the light.

She ran her fingers across his face, like a blind woman learning braille. Prominent cheekbones, bold brow, features Eric had taken from Sully's gene pool. Sully's nose had a small bump on the bridge...the remnant of a break that had occurred his first year on the police force.

It was a face that Theresa loved...a face that would only grow more handsome with age. She saw the shadows of Sully's face each time she looked at Eric.

A sob caught in her throat, and Sully pulled her to him. With her cheek against the warmth of his chest, she could hear his heartbeat, a thundering pulse that had often lulled her to sleep when they were married. She'd missed that...the metronome of his heartbeat.

She tangled her fingers in his chest hair, felt the stir of his desire against her thigh. She knew Sully's desire was more than physical. She saw his need shining in the depths of his tear-filled eyes, the hunger of the soul to connect intimately with the mother of his missing child.

She reached her hand down and stroked the length of him, remembering the night she believed their lovemaking had resulted in Eric's conception.

It had been the night of their six-month anniversary. She'd surprised him with a night in a luxury hotel room. They'd stayed in bed all night and most of the next morning, finally hurrying to dress minutes before checkout time. It had been a night of love, a recommitment of the vows they'd spoken six months before. Two months later, when she discovered herself pregnant, she'd known that particular night of love had produced the legacy she carried inside her.

A fresh wave of emotion swept through her with the memories. That had been a time of innocence, when they were young enough to believe that good always overcomes evil and their love was strong enough to survive any bumps life threw in their path.

She kissed him again, knowing that this time it was her own tears she tasted.

SULLY DRANK of Theresa's kiss, as if her lips alone possessed the elixir to heal the wound Eric's absence left behind. He tangled his hands in her hair...dark silk with a touch of red in the sunlight...so like Eric's.

In all the hours of his deepest despair, in all the agony of self-doubt and loss of himself, Sully had never felt the kind of yawning anguish he felt when Donny told him the money was gone. And along with the money had gone their hopes for finding Eric.

He stroked Theresa's breast, wanting to lose himself in desire, allow the flames of passion to momentarily hush the horror in his mind. He wanted to warm himself, cloak himself with her, allow them to give a small measure of comfort to one another.

He rolled her on her back, her hair splaying out against the bold geometric-patterned rug. Leaning his head down, he touched his mouth to her nipple, heard the swift intake of her breath as the pinkish tip grew taut.

He not only wanted to love her body, he wanted to embrace her soul, give to her, in an effort to appease the hunger they both felt for their child. In this despair, they were united, and it seemed only right that they comfort each other by the most intimate communication a man and a woman could have...by making love.

As he caressed her breasts with his lips, his hand

sought the damp heat between her thighs. She gasped and arched up to meet his intimate touch.

The blue of her eyes deepened to navy, glazed with a familiar look. He knew the pleasure of his touch was driving all other conscious thought from her mind. That was what he wanted...to give her heart, her very soul, a respite from the darkness.

He increased the depth and length of his caresses, wanting to sweep her away from the tree with no angel, the house with no laughter, the home with no child.

Her responses, the little sounds she made, all were as familiar to him as the back of his own hand, the sight of his face in the mirror, and yet each moan, every caress she returned, felt as new, as exciting, as it had the very first time they made love.

As her hand curled around him, her touch as intimate as his on her, he felt the last of his rational thought slipping away beneath a mountain of emotion too complicated to sort through.

Much later, he picked her up in his arms and carried her into her bedroom. He helped her pull a nightgown over her head, then tucked her in beneath the sheets. He could tell that she was empty...bereft of thought, energy and emotion.

The emotional stress of the past three days, the nights of little sleep, had finally caught up with her, and almost immediately she fell into a deep, soundless sleep.

Sully sat in a chair at the side of the bed, watching her sleep. Occasionally her eyelids quivered and her forehead wrinkled. Nightmares, he thought. Even in sleep, the strain didn't ease.

As he continued to watch her, his heart filled with love for her. He loved her...had never stopped loving her. But it was only now, while she slept, that he allowed himself to feel it, to embrace the love he felt for her.

She and Eric had been everything good in his life up until the time of his shooting. She'd been his laughter, his joy, his passion. He'd marveled at her intelligence, delighted in her wit. Theirs had been a charmed existence, made only more wonderful with Eric's birth.

Having grown up with an alcoholic father, before meeting Theresa, Sully had believed that happiness was for everyone else, but not in his cards. Theresa had brought him a happiness he'd never dreamed possible.

The night of his shooting, it had all shattered, and he'd realized then that fate had been laughing at him. Fate had taunted him by showing him a glimpse of happiness, then snatched it all away.

He'd picked up his first glass of booze to ease some of the physical pain the bullet had left behind. He'd found a seductive side effect. It had also numbed the emotional pain of knowing he'd never again be the man he'd been, and he'd never again be anyone's hero.

He remembered the look in his mother's eyes when his father would come home drunk once again. Pity coupled with revulsion. Sully supposed his mother had loved his father once, but years of disappointments and empty promises had destroyed that love. Sully hadn't wanted that to happen to him and Theresa. He'd never wanted to see that pity, that revulsion, in Theresa's eyes, so he'd left.

He could love her now, while she slept, because in sleep he felt no demands from her. When she was awake, he felt the weight of expectations he could never fulfill. Yes, he could love her while she slept, but when she awakened he'd have to push that emotion aside, forget it ever existed.

It was nearly three o'clock when he pulled himself out of the chair in the bedroom and went into the living room. He knew sleep would be impossible, as his mind kept going over and over the events of the past three days.

The police had exhausted all clues. The list of potential suspects had become nonexistent. Sully still had the feeling that Eric's disappearance wasn't a stranger abduction, but had been executed by somebody Theresa and Sully knew. He had the same sick feeling in his gut that he'd had on the night he got out of his patrol car and advanced into that alley.

He had nothing to base his feeling on, other than the instincts honed through years of police work, and he no longer knew if they could be trusted.

And what really bothered him was a deep-down feeling that his shooting and Eric's disappearance were somehow related. But that didn't make sense...did it?

As always, when he tried to focus on that night so

long ago, a sick unease swept through him. Something nibbled at the edges of his mind...a forgotten detail...a suppressed memory that Sully suspected held an important clue to exactly what had happened that night.

As the nighttime hours slipped away, Sully sat and stared at the Christmas tree, trying to retrieve whatever it was that might be hidden in the dark recesses of his mind.

By six o'clock, he was no closer to any answers. But he knew what had to be done. He left a note for Theresa on the pillow next to hers, then crept out of the house.

No dawn light broke the gray shroud of morning. Clouds hung heavy and full, laden with the promise of snow. A cold northern wind whipped through him as he ran to his car.

No press awaited him. The sidewalk outside was empty. It was Christmas morning. All but the most dedicated journalists would be home with their families. Those working would eventually come back here—the story was too heartbreaking, too rich with emotion, to ignore.

As he waited for his engine to warm, he stared at the house, outlined with the red and green lights that blinked a beacon of hope.

Christmas morning. In several of the houses down the block, already lights were turning on. Sully knew children lived in these homes, children who couldn't wait for a reasonable hour, who awoke early in excitement and anticipation of the treasures Santa had left behind.

Eric had always been an early riser on Christmas morning. "Santa came! Santa came!" His excited voice would awaken Theresa and Sully. He'd jump into the middle of their bed, his little body toasty with sleep, his cheeks ruddy with excitement. "Come on...get up! Santa came!"

Sully's hands tightened around the steering wheel at the sweet memory. Where was Eric? Where in the hell was his son?

He put the car in drive and pulled away from the curb. If Eric was still alive, then time was of the essence. Whether it was stranger abduction or acquaintance kidnapping, keeping a child of Eric's age and intelligence captive would quickly become too great a task. Time was running out. Sully just hoped it hadn't already run out.

Chapter Twelve

December 25

Theresa awoke at a few minutes before seven, her eyelids swollen from the deep sleep that had possessed her for the past several hours.

Although she should have felt somewhat refreshed, she didn't. She felt dull, lifeless and still so afraid. She knew without opening her eyes that Sully wasn't in the bed next to her. His body warmth was gone, and the room held only the sounds of her own breathing.

She squeezed her eyes tightly closed. Why get up? What reason did she have to get out of bed? It was Christmas morning, but no joy awaited her. Without Eric, she'd never have Christmas again.

Theresa had never known hatred before, but God help her, as she lay in bed, listening to the sound of emptiness in this house bereft of Eric, she hated the person responsible. She hoped he was arrested, thrown in prison for the rest of his natural life.

She rolled over on her back and stared up at the

ceiling, thinking of those moments of give-and-take, the communication of hearts, that had happened when she and Sully made love. Still, even as intimately as they touched one another, as close as she felt to him in those moments, she'd felt a distance she couldn't breach, a place in his heart she couldn't touch.

She'd thought she was over Sully. She'd believed she'd put him into her past as efficiently as she'd placed her wedding band in a safety-deposit box. But their lovemaking last night had been more than a physical joining. He'd touched her soul, curled himself forever around her heart. He'd left her past and reminded her that now, as much as ever, she loved him. But to what avail?

She rolled over on her other side, her hand slapping against a piece of paper on the opposite pillow. She picked it up and scanned it, unsurprised that Sully had left to take a drive. He'd never done well in the patient-waiting department. And this house without Eric would drive him as crazy as it drove her.

She spied the shirt he'd worn the day before at the end of the bed. On impulse, she leaned down, grabbed it and pulled it on around her thin nightgown.

Instantly she was engulfed in the scent of Sully, a spicy, earthy smell that comforted her. She pulled it tight around herself and lay down again.

She knew what she was doing—focusing on her relationship, or lack of one, with Sully, in order to keep her mind away from the horror of Eric's absence.

Eric. *Where are you, baby?* She believed what she'd told Sully, that someplace Eric was still alive.

She should get up. Theresa had never been one to laze in bed after awakening. She'd always prided herself on being a go-getter, greeting each day eagerly, ready to brand her mark on the world. Sully used to tease her, telling her that if he wanted to make love to his wife in the mornings, he usually had to go chase her down.

Yes, she should get up...but why?

Donny and Kip and the rest of the officers probably wouldn't be here until later in the day. Theresa suspected they believed that the ransom demand had been a hoax that paid off for some sicko, that whoever collected that money hadn't had Eric at all. So where was he? Where was her baby?

For the first time in her life, Theresa didn't want to get out of bed. Instead, she closed her eyes once again, reaching...seeking the dark oblivion of her sleep.

Within minutes, she'd fallen into a beautiful dream. The sun was shining and she and Sully and Eric were playing in a park. She could smell the sweet scent of the bright green grass, hear the boyish joy of Eric's laughter mingling with Sully's deeper, richer laughter as they tossed a Frisbee back and forth.

In some deep part of her consciousness, she was aware that it was a dream, but she didn't care. They were together, and Eric's laughter rode the summer breeze.

When Sully gazed at her, his eyes were filled with the kind of love, the promise and commitment, they had radiated with on the day Sully and Theresa were wed. His smile warmed her, stoked a fire of desire, of love, inside her.

A loud bang resounded, and the beautiful vision shimmered, like a picture dropped to the floor. Another bang, and Sully's image faded away. "No!" Theresa cried mournfully. The third bang made Eric vanish, as if he'd never existed...leaving Theresa alone...sobbing in despair as the warm summer breeze turned to arctic winds of ice.

She sat up, realized the banging in her dreams was somebody knocking at her back door. She got out of bed and pulled a robe on over her nightgown and Sully's shirt. Swiping the tears from her cheeks, she hurried to the back door.

"Theresa." Rose's plump arms wound around Theresa, pulling her against Rose's broad body as the older woman burst into tears.

"It's all right, Rose. Shhh..." Theresa found it odd that she should be the one comforting. She looked helplessly at Vincent, who stood behind his wife, as Rose's sobs rose in volume and pitch.

"She's been doing that since we left St. Louis," Vincent said, his dark eyes radiating his innate kindness, along with grief for the little boy he'd grown to love.

"Rose..." Theresa extracted herself from the

woman's embrace and motioned them both into the warmth of the kitchen.

"We got here as soon as we could," Vincent explained as he shrugged out of his overcoat. "We would have been here sooner, but we didn't know."

"We didn't know until the police knocked on our hotel room door. There we were, in the honeymoon suite, having a little champagne, not knowing that our little boy was in trouble." Wails of anguish once again racked Rose's body. "And those police officers...so suspicious, looking in the room...in our car."

Rose looked at Theresa, a touch of betrayal in her dark eyes. "How could you think...even for a moment...that Vincent...that I could have anything to do with this? That we could hurt Eric...or you?" Tears oozed from her eyes and ran unchecked down her plump cheeks.

"I'm sorry." Theresa's voice was faint, filled with the heartbreak she felt not only for herself, but for these two people who had been her friends, the friendship now tainted with the cloud of suspicion. "We had to check everyone.... You weren't home, and that was unusual, and I'm sorry, Rose...Vincent."

She looked from one to the other, and inwardly cursed the person who had not only taken Eric, but had torn apart the very fabric of her life, stuck holes in friendships where none had existed before.

Even if Eric was delivered back home safe and sound in the next moment, nothing in Theresa's life would ever be the same again. Truths had been exposed, weaknesses magnified, beneath the stress of Eric's disappearance. And as she looked at Vincent and Rose, she wondered if one of the casualties of the case would be their friendship.

"I would face the devil himself to find out where that boy is," Rose said as she opened her purse and withdrew a tissue.

She mopped at her cheeks, then covered Theresa's hand with hers. "And I would give the police my own mother if I thought there was even the most remote chance that it would help to find my child. How can I fault you for doing much the same?"

"We're here to help, Theresa," Vincent said. "You and Eric are like family, the only family Rose and I have. Tell us what we can do, and we'll do it. Anything...anything at all."

Theresa looked at the two older people, her heart swelling at the magnitude of their friendship. They had been roused from a second honeymoon, their joyous holiday trip destroyed by the grimness of life and ugly suspicions. But Vincent and Rose held no grudge, only love for her and her son.

Tears blurred Theresa's vision as she squeezed tightly to Rose's hand. "There's only one thing left for us all to do where Eric is concerned...."

"Anything," Rose said without hesitation.

"Whatever we can do," Vincent replied.

"Pray," Theresa said softly. "There's nothing left to be done but wait...and pray."

SULLY PARKED HIS CAR down the street from the alley where eighteen months ago he'd nearly died. It had begun to snow, the flakes spotting his windshield like icy starbursts.

In this part of town, there was less indication of the holiday. No colorful Christmas lights outlined the abandoned warehouses and low-income apartment buildings. No fancy plastic wreaths or smiling Santas adorned the lawns or waved from rooftops.

Still, several apartment windows were filled with small Christmas trees with sparkling lights, and he knew that in those apartments the morning joy would be no less great than in homes everywhere else in the city. Joy and good cheer everywhere...except in his house.

He should be home with Theresa. This morning would be the most difficult she'd ever faced. Christmas morning without Eric. Yes, he should be there for her. So, what was he doing sitting in his car on the wrong side of town, with snow slowly obscuring his view?

In truth, he wasn't sure what he was doing here. He only knew he needed to be here. Somehow he felt as if the events of the past and the events of the present had merged, were connected in some obscene, crazy way.

He got out of the car, the snowflakes big and fluffy and melting immediately as they hit the warmth of his face. Please...please don't let Eric be out in the cold, out in the snow, he prayed.

Leaning against the front of his car, he fought an

eddying, nauseating fear as he gazed up the street to the mouth of the alley.

It was the landscape of his nightmares, the source of his night terrors. He didn't want to go back there, didn't want to relive that night.

But he knew he would do just that. If there was a chance in hell that he might come up with something, any clue to help find Eric, he'd brave his personal demons in this place of his spiritual death.

Sully tensed as he saw a man approaching. Who on earth would be out at this time of the morning in this weather? He relaxed as he realized the man was delivering morning newspapers from a large bag he carried.

"Got an extra one of those?" Sully asked when he drew closer.

"Sure." The answer came with a grin and a puff of white air. He held out a paper to Sully, who took it, then dug into his pocket for some money. "Here, don't worry about it," the man said. "This one's on me. Merry Christmas." With a wave and another grin, he continued on his route.

Sully took the paper and got back into his car. He wasn't surprised to find Eric's photo in the center of the front page. Where Is Eric? The headline read. A smaller photo of Donny accompanied the article.

Sully scanned it briefly. Amazing. Donny made it sound as if although the child was still missing, the police were on top of things and expected a happy result at any moment.

Donny was nothing if not a savvy politician. If

Chief Lewis really did retire, Donny would be a good replacement. Sully closed the paper and threw it into the back of the car.

Getting out of the car once again, he pulled his collar up around his neck, ducked his head against the wind and blowing snow, then walked toward the alley.

With every step that brought him closer, dread built until it filled his chest like the weight of pneumonia. Again he had the feeling of some memory flirting with the edges of his consciousness, darting just out of reach when he thought it might be grasped.

He reached the mouth of the alley and stopped, pausing to draw in deep gulps of the cold air. What the hell was he doing here? He should be home with Theresa...waiting to discover what leads the police were following. But he knew those thoughts were the rationalization of a coward, and he couldn't afford to be a coward now...not with Eric's life on the line.

Although he knew it was impossible, as Sully walked into the alley, he imagined he could smell the scent of rotting garbage, feel the steamy heat of a summer night surrounding him and radiating upward from the pavement.

His heart pumped the rhythm of panic, but he tamped the fear down as he approached the place where Louie had died, the place where he'd nearly lost his own life.

When he reached the spot, he turned and scanned the windows around him, finally focusing on the second floor window of the building to his right. That was where the shooter had stood, at the broken window of the abandoned warehouse. There, he'd taken careful aim and snuffed out Louie with a single shot. Then, aiming once again, he'd tried to kill Sully... and nearly succeeded.

He dusted the gathering snow off the top of one of the steel trash cans and sat...waiting. Seconds passed...minutes. The snow continued to fall, and Sully continued to wait.

With each minute that passed, his despair grew deeper, his grief more profound. He'd expected a miracle. He'd hoped for an epiphany to unfold the truth of what had really happened that night. He'd hoped for some answers that might lead to Eric.

But it wasn't happening. No sudden vision to display the truth. No moment of clarity to explain anything. Nothing. The only thing he felt was bone-chilling cold and the realization that this alley no longer evoked his fear. Like a child realizing with the light of day that the scary shadows weren't really monsters, Sully knew that his fear of this place would no longer hold him captive in nightmares.

He needed to get home to Theresa. He'd been a fool to think he could gain any answers here. Theresa would need him, and for once in his life Sully wanted to be there for her.

Rising from the trash can, he felt as if in the past several minutes he'd aged a dozen years. He'd come here seeking answers, wanting a clue...a memory that might help him discover who had his son.

Maybe the chief had been right all along. Nobody had set him up, nobody had betrayed him. He'd just been in the wrong place at the wrong time. The incident eighteen months ago had nothing to do with Eric's disappearance.

As he stepped out of the alley, a car whizzed by, and in that instant Sully had the answers he'd sought. The memory that had eluded him blossomed in his head, filling him with surprise, then a rage so intense he fought for self-control.

He'd been right. All along, he'd been right. He'd been set up. And now, although he didn't know the why...he knew the who, and his knowledge burned inside him, along with the need for vengeance.

He got into his car and drove to the first pay phone he saw, his anger a living, breathing entity inside him. He dug in his pockets, found a quarter, fed it into the phone, then punched in seven numbers.

"Meet me at the Shady Tree Apartments, number 302," he said to the voice who'd answered.

"But that's—"

"I know who lives there," Sully said, interrupting. "If I'm right, I need your help. If I'm wrong, then you'll need to arrest me." Without waiting for any reply, Sully hung up and got back into his car.

ERIC KNEW IT WAS MORNING. He could see the faint gray light seeping in around the edges of the boards at the window. Christmas morning...and the only gift he wanted was to be home with his mom and dad.

Tears burned at his eyes, but he swallowed them

away. He didn't have time to cry right now. For some reason, his mom and dad and the police hadn't been able to find him. Eric knew it was up to him to get out of here, and the only way out was through the window.

Quickly, not wanting to wait a moment longer, he pried off the loose bottom board. Snow. It was snowing outside. Big, fluffy flakes that were already turning the ground from brown to white. The window behind the boards was cracked, and through that crack he could smell the snow, the fresh scent welcome after the staleness of the room.

For a single moment, he allowed excitement to flow through him. Gosh, he loved snow. When he got home, he'd see if his mom would help him make a snowman. Or, if it snowed enough he'd build a whole snow fort in the backyard. He smiled at the thought, the smile fading as he realized that first he had to get out of this cellar.

His fingers were still sore from all the work he'd done yesterday, but he ignored the stinging fingertips as he pried at the second board.

Sometimes Joe's teammates couldn't help him, and it was up to him to scramble for extra yardage, make the first down all alone. That was what Eric was doing now...scrambling all alone.

He gasped in surprise when the second board finally broke loose and fell to the floor. Now there was a space big enough for him to crawl through. All he had to do was break out the window.

Knowing better than to use his hand to break out

the window, he instead used his elbow, knowing his thick coat would keep him from being cut. It took him four tries before the window finally shattered and clean, cold air poured through the opening.

Carefully he picked the pieces that remained out of the frame, then jumped up and crawled out the small space. He found himself at the back of an old house. Thick woods surrounded the house, and Eric looked around curiously. He had no idea where he was, which way might be home.

He crept up the side of the house, toward the front, then darted behind a small evergreen tree when he heard the sound of a car approaching. Was it the masked man returning? What would he do when he found Eric gone? Eric looked toward the woods. Too late to run now. If he did, whoever was driving that car would see him.

As the car came into full view, joy burst inside Eric, taking the place of his fear. He knew that car. It belonged to one of his dad's friends...a policeman. Eric frowned, wishing he could remember the man's name. It didn't matter. He would take Eric home... home to his mom and dad. Everything was going to be okay.

Tears spilled down Eric's cheeks as he realized it was over. He was finally going home.

The car parked in front of the house, and Eric stood up from his hiding place. He watched as the tall man got out of the car. "Hey...here I am! I'm here!" Eric cried with excitement.

The man turned to face him, and in his hand Eric

saw that he gripped a ski mask. Cold terror reached down Eric's throat and enclosed his heart in a painful grasp.

This man wasn't a friend. He hadn't come to help. This was the man who'd brought him here...the bad man.

"Eric." Surprise twisted the man's features. "What are you doing out here?"

Without answering, without hesitation, Eric took off running for the woods.

"Eric. Come back here. Dammit, stop running right now." The man's voice was filled with anger.

Eric didn't stop. He ran as fast as his legs could carry him. The man was running now, too. Running fast and cursing as he chased Eric.

"Eric, there's nothing to be afraid about. Just stop a minute and everything will be just fine."

Lies. All lies. Eric sobbed, his chest on fire, as he continued to run. It wouldn't be long and he'd be out of breath, unable to run any farther. And Eric knew with certainty that if the man caught him, he'd never, ever, see his mom and dad again.

Chapter Thirteen

Sully drove toward the Shady Tree Apartments with a burning in his gut, a hole in his heart. There was a part of him that hoped that the final piece of memory that had clicked into place was false. He didn't want to believe what he'd remembered, didn't want to believe that a man he'd trusted, a man who'd been his fraternal brother, would so betray him.

But he knew that wasn't the case. Still, there could be a logical explanation, some reasonable interpretation, to what Sully believed he'd seen that night just before walking into the alley.

Be home, he prayed as he parked in the lot of the apartment building. Please, be home and tell me I'm wrong. Tell me you didn't betray me eighteen months ago, and tell me you had nothing to do with Eric's disappearance.

Sully gave himself no chance for doubts, no opportunity to second-guess the instincts that now roared inside him like an animal struggling to survive. Without hesitation, he got out of the car and entered the building.

Upon entering, he was faced with stairs going up and a staircase going down. He took the stairs up two at a time, knowing that apartment 302 was the second door on the left.

When he reached the door, he knocked boldly, loud enough to awaken anyone asleep inside. No answer. Exactly what he'd anticipated. He tried the doorknob, also unsurprised to find it locked. Nobody home.

He touched the door, knowing that what he was about to do next would make him cross a line, put him on the side of the criminals instead of the side of angels. But it also just might save his son's life.

Taking two steps backward, he focused all his energy into his leg as he punched the door with his foot, right next to the doorknob. He heard the telltale crackle of wood and lock disengaging. One more good shot should do it. He hit it once again, springing the door open.

"Sully, what in the hell are you doing?" Kip hurried down the hallway toward him.

"I think it's called breaking and entering." Sully started into the apartment, but Kip stopped him by grabbing him by the arm.

"You want to tell me what the hell is going on?" Kip's frustration showed in the heightened color of his cheeks, the angry sparkle in his eyes. "Have you gone around the bend, or what?"

The door across the hall opened, and a tiny old woman peered out, her pink curlers looking like antennas. "Official police business, ma'am," Kip said, displaying his badge. She slammed her door, and Kip pulled Sully into the apartment Sully had just broken into. "Now, want to tell me what's going on?" He glared at Sully.

"Holbrook was there...the night I was shot."

"What?" Kip's eyes widened in surprise. "But he went home sick that day."

"He wasn't home sick. He was there."

"How do you know?"

"I went back to the alley a little earlier this morning. I hadn't been back there since that night. I remembered, Kip. I remember seeing his car parked down the street. Not many of those bright yellow Corvettes around town. He was supposed to be here, with the flu, but he wasn't. He was waiting for me. He set the whole thing up, and now I think he's got Eric."

"No. Surely you're mistaken, Sully." Kip leaned against the door, his eyes filled with disbelief. "Why? Why would Donny do anything like that?"

"I don't know why," Sully admitted. "If I'm wrong, then you can arrest me for breaking and entering. But if I'm right, then there might be a clue to where Eric is in this apartment."

"We should get a search warrant."

Sully frowned with impatience. "You know that would take forever, and besides, nobody is going to issue a warrant based on my gut instinct and memory."

Kip studied Sully for a long moment, his intelligent, piercing eyes seeming to weigh and judge not only what Sully had said, but Sully the man, as well.

Sully found himself holding his breath, realizing how important it was that Kip believe him, trust his instincts, the instincts Sully had thought he'd lost.

"Then I guess we'd better get looking, shouldn't we?" Kip said.

Sully closed his eyes, gratefulness causing emotion to grow thick in his throat. "Thank you," he finally managed to say.

"You know where Donny is now?" Kip asked as he began in one corner of the living room and Sully started searching the other side of the room.

"I hoped he'd be here. I hoped he'd be here and tell me something to prove me wrong," Sully said as he took the cushions off the sofa and checked beneath them.

The apartment was obviously that of a single guy, not overly clean, but neat. There were not many knickknacks, no personal pictures on the wall, no feminine touches to make the apartment a warm, inviting home.

"Maybe you just missed him. Maybe he's at your place now."

"That's the next place I'll look for him...after I check every nook and cranny here."

They worked silently, methodically, making sure that everything was put back the way they had found it. Sully wanted to rip the place apart, destroy anything that belonged to Donny, but he kept his rage in check, knowing he had to be smarter than his anger.

Sully knew Kip was taking a big chance, risking dismissal and loss of his pension and retirement by participating in this illegal search.

Sully also knew that part of what motivated Kip was not only the thought of a missing child, but the hope that somehow their search would prove Donny innocent of Sully's suspicions.

The living room yielded nothing, no indication at all that Donny had anything to do with Eric's disappearance. Nor did the kitchen hold any clues. It wasn't until Sully dug through the kitchen garbage that he came up with a receipt from a convenience store that made his heart pound. "Why would Donny, on the day that Eric disappeared, buy sandwiches, potato chips, soda and comic books?"

"Who knows? Maybe he was hungry and he's not into heavy reading material." Kip straightened from the cabinet under the sink. "Sully, you can't jump to conclusions. It's just a damned receipt."

Sully knew Kip was right. He couldn't explain how certain he was that Donny had set him up to die and that now Donny had orchestrated Eric's disappearance. The receipt gave him hope. If Donny had Eric, and if this receipt was an indication, then at least he hadn't killed Eric. He'd bought food and entertainment, and that implied he meant to keep Eric alive. Damn, but there were so many ifs...and no matter how he told himself the receipt might be a good sign, his stomach rolled and bucked with fear.

"You want to know what scares the hell out of me?" Sully looked at Kip, needing to say the words, needing to share the horror that had gripped him from the moment he remembered Donny's car being parked down the street from that alley. "If Donny is capable of standing in a window, aiming his gun at me and pulling the trigger, then what's he capable of doing to my son?"

Kip's eyes darkened. "Come on, let's go check the bedroom."

Although it had only taken them minutes to search the living room and kitchen, Sully had the feeling of time racing while he moved in slow motion. If they could just find something, anything that would tie Donny to Eric, anything that would give a hint of where Eric might be being held.

"Son of a..."

"What?" Sully raced over to where Kip stood at the closet door. He peered inside the small closet and there, on the floor, spied what had caused Kip's exclamation. A brown paper sack, identical to the one Sully had stuffed with the ransom money. Sully leaned down and opened the sack, exposing the money for Kip to see.

"Okay, so now we know if nothing else Donny is a dirty cop," Kip said. "Maybe he just intended to cash in on a bad situation."

Sully picked up an item from the closet floor next to the paper sack. It was a battery operated toy, a voice synethisizer that transformed an ordinary tone into a roboticlike speech.

"He's a dirty cop who tried to kill me, and now has my son." Sully hit the closet door with his fist, the sound thundering through the small apartment. "But where? Where in the hell would he have him?"

"Sully?" Kip frowned thoughtfully. "A couple of weeks ago Donny was complaining because the taxes were due on his father's old farmhouse. He'd been hoping to sell it, but from what I gathered it was in pretty bad shape."

"Yeah...yeah, I remember Donny talking about his dad's place before his dad died." Sully tried to reach back into his memory, back to the days when he and Donny had ridden together as partners.

Donny's father had been an invalid in the last couple years of his life, and Donny had often complained about the time he had to spend on his days off at the farm. But where was the farm? Sully knew it wasn't too far from here, but where, exactly?

"I could find it by computer," Kip said. "Let me go home, and I'll access tax files, find it that way."

"Come on, it's quicker to go to Theresa's. She's got a computer with a modem, you can do it there. Grab that sack. We'll take it back to Theresa, and she can give it back to the bank."

"What happens when Donny discovers it's missing?"

Sully smiled tightly. "What's he going to do? File a police report?"

Kip hesitated a moment, then nodded and grabbed the sack, and together he and Sully left the apartment. As Sully drove to Theresa's house, with Kip following in his own car, Sully's thoughts went to the man who'd been his partner.

What haunted Sully at the moment was why...why would Donny want him dead? Why would Donny want to hurt him enough to steal his son?

There had never been a hint of any ill feelings between the two men. For two years, they had been partners. They'd shared pieces of themselves, faced tough situations together. Sully had trusted Donny to watch his back, to be there for him when the heat was on, and that only made the betrayal more bitter.

There were no doubts in Sully's mind now. It had been the sight of his partner's distinctive yellow sports car parked down the street that caused the premonition of doom, the strange unease that coursed through Sully as he headed down that alley.

Somehow, in the aftermath of the shooting, that memory had been repressed, shoved into a dark corner of his mind. Sully's feeling that he'd been set up had been right, but after the shooting he hadn't been able to remember the sight of Donny's car.

Donny had to be crazy—that was the only explanation. He must possess some sort of madness in his soul, a madness he'd been able to keep secret until that hot summer night so long ago. A secret madness. A killing madness.

Sully stepped on the accelerator, once again feeling the press of time passing...with Eric's life in the balance.

THERESA FINALLY got Vincent and Rose to go home, after assuring them a dozen times that she'd call them if there was any news at all.

After they left, Theresa dressed and sank down on the sofa, her gaze focused on the Christmas tree. Her heart cried out soundlessly, the pain too deep for words as she stared at the empty space at the top…the visual reminder that Eric wasn't home.

When she could stand the sight of the tree no longer, she moved to the kitchen, where she made a fresh pot of coffee, then stood at the window and watched it snow.

The weather service had indicated that the area was under a winter storm warning, with expected snow totals of six to twelve inches and winds between thirty and fifty miles an hour.

Wherever Eric was…she hoped it was someplace warm and dry. His coat wasn't thick enough for him to endure this kind of cold for long, and as usual, he'd forgotten his gloves that morning when he left for school.

That morning. Oh, how she wished she could call it back. How she wished she had driven him to school or kept him home that day. How she wished she could turn back the hands of time and stop all this from happening.

She jumped when the back door flew open and Sully and Kip walked in.

"Your computer. Kip needs to use it," Sully said, his tone sharp.

"In the back bedroom. Why? What's happened? What's going on?" She followed the two men down the hallway and into the bedroom office, where Kip sat down in the chair at the desk and turned on the computer.

"I think Donny has Eric," Sully said.

"What?" she gasped. "But, Sully, why? My God, that doesn't make any sense!"

"I know it doesn't. But it's what I believe." He looked at her, his eyes dark with torment. "He shot me, Theresa. That night in the alley, he stood in a window and aimed his gun. It was Donny who tried to kill me."

"Oh, Sully." She leaned weakly against the wall, trying to comprehend, to make sense of it all. "Are you positive it was him?"

Sully touched his chest, the place where Theresa knew the doctors had removed a bullet, a place that still bore the scar of that night. "I've never been so sure. I...I don't know why he did it, but I know that he did. And I think he's got our son."

"My God, if what you say is true, then Donny is a monster." Anger stirred, a bubbling cauldron of rage that filled her, momentarily sweeping away the emptiness, the fear. "He sat with us, at our table, in our home...for the last three days he's watched our terror, seen our torment. What kind of a monster does something like that?" She drew in a deep breath to steady her raging emotions. "What's Kip doing?"

"If Holbrook is a monster, then he has to have a lair. That's what I'm looking for," Kip explained as his fingers nimbly punched the keyboard.

"Donny's father had a farm on the outskirts of town. Kip's trying to find out the exact location."

"And you think Eric might be there?" Theresa's heart thundered in her chest.

"If Donny has him...that's where he'll be," Sully said with finality.

"Bingo," Kip cried in triumph. "County tax records show one Donald Holbrook paid taxes on a piece of property just outside city limits on the south side of town—2900 Highway 10."

"I'm on my way." Sully started out the door.

"Sully, wait!" Kip yelled after him. Both Theresa and Kip hurried after Sully, catching up to him at the front door. "You can't go out there all alone," Kip said.

"He won't be alone. I'm going with him." Theresa pulled her coat from the hall closet.

"Theresa..." Sully began.

She held up a hand to still him. "Don't tell me to stay here, Sully. Don't you even try to talk me into not going with you." She held his gaze, determinedly, defiantly. There was no way in hell he was going to talk her into staying here while he went to the place where their son might be.

"It could be dangerous," he said.

"I know that." She buttoned her coat. "Now let's go."

"I'll get backup and meet you out there," Kip said.

"Don't use your radio," Sully warned. "Donny might be monitoring." Sully grabbed Theresa's arm. "Come on, let's go get our son."

Chapter Fourteen

Wind buffeted the car and howled around the windows like a mourning banshee. The blowing and falling snow not only cut down visibility to almost nothing, but also made for excruciatingly slow going.

Theresa stared out the window, feeling as if Mother Nature were conspiring with Donny to keep her away from her son. She wrapped her arms around herself and moved the heater vent to blow directly on her.

"How far do we have to go?" she asked Sully, whose knuckles shone white as he fought to keep the car on the road.

"About fifteen miles, but it's impossible for me to go much faster than thirty. Damn, if only this snow had held off for another hour or two."

"It doesn't matter how long it takes us to get there. Either we get there in time...or we don't."

Sully looked at her sharply, and she held his gaze for a long moment. She knew there were no guarantees of what they would find at the farmhouse. There was no guarantee Eric would be there...and if he was, there was no guarantee he'd still be alive. She closed her eyes for a moment, rejecting the possibility.

Sully reached out and touched her hand, a touch that communicated strength and the commitment to do whatever was in his power to make Eric be safe. But Theresa knew Eric's safety was not in their hands. It was in the hands of a man they had trusted, a man they'd thought a friend, an utter madman.

"How did you remember that Donny was there the night you were shot?" she asked as he released her hand and gripped the steering wheel once again.

"I knew there was something about that night I wasn't remembering, some detail that kept niggling at the back of my mind." He kept his focus on the city streets. "I was up all night, thinking about it, wondering about it, and somehow in my gut I believed that Eric's disappearance and my shooting were connected."

Theresa held her breath as they turned a corner and the back end of the car spun out, nearly sending them headfirst into a street sign. Sully backed off the gas and whirled the steering wheel, managing to right the car on the icy street.

"Close call," she said, relaxing her death grip on the dashboard. She stared out the window, where the road seemed to have disappeared beneath the blanket of snow. "Will we be able to make it to the farmhouse?"

He flashed her a tight smile. "If I have to steal a bulldozer, eventually we'll make it."

They didn't speak again until they left the city streets and turned onto Highway 10. Here, the road conditions were even worse. With no buildings, no obstacles to block the wind, the snow blew and drifted on the roadway, making traveling not only difficult, but hazardous.

"I went back to the alley this morning," Sully said as he slowed the car to a crawl. "I hadn't been there since the night of the shooting."

"Oh, Sully, I know how difficult it must have been for you to go back to that place." Theresa remembered what Kip had told her, about the fear that Sully had suffered since the night of the shooting, a fear he'd suffered all alone.

She studied his features, the taut line of his jaw, the deep shadows both in and below his eyes. She remembered the nightmares he'd suffered, his silence and withdrawal after that night. "Why didn't you tell me all the things you were thinking, feeling, after the shooting?" she asked softly.

For a long moment, the only sound in the car was the hum of the heater fan and the rhythmic swish-swish of the windshield-wiper blades.

"It was all so ugly," he finally said. "I was angry, and filled with fear and suspicions." He shot a quick glance to her. "I didn't want to taint you with that."

Theresa's heart filled with love for this man who'd suffered alone, afraid to expose his fears to her. And again she wondered what they'd done wrong, what ingredient their marriage had lacked, that he didn't feel he could come to her, share the bad along with the good.

She stared back out the window, the cold, desolate wind outside having nothing on the one that blew through her heart. She'd lost Sully long ago. Was Eric lost to her, as well?

"I still don't understand any of this. Why would Donny want to set you up? Had you been fighting with him before the night of the shooting? Did something happen that might have made him so angry?" She looked once again at Sully.

"I wish I had those answers, Theresa, but I don't. I've thought about it and thought about it, but Donny and I were fine up until the moment he shot me. We never exchanged a cross word with one another. And I've scarcely seen him since the shooting, so I can't imagine what prompted him to take Eric."

"But you're sure he did."

Sully nodded. "We found a voice synthesizer in Donny's closet, along with the ransom money." Sully hit the steering wheel with the palm of his hand. "I wondered when we got the note and the ransom phone call if the house was being watched, because the calls came in when Donny wasn't at our house. I should have known then something was screwy."

"How could you know that the man running the kidnap investigation was the kidnapper himself?"

"I should have known. The moment we got the note, it should have been handed over to the FBI, but it wasn't." His voice was filled with torment. "I should have pieced it all together.'' He hesitated a moment, then added. ''If I hadn't been such a coward, I would have gone back to that alley sooner, realized that Donny had tried to kill me. Then none of this with Eric would be happening.''

His words sent a torrent of shock through Theresa. ''My God, Sully. You can't blame yourself for this.'' She reached over and touched his arm, felt the tautness of muscle, the tension that radiated from him. ''Sully, Donny is crazy, the most insidious kind of crazy of all, because he managed to hide it from everyone. By taking even partial blame for this, you diminish his guilt. He's the guilty one, Sully, not you.''

He acknowledged her words with a curt nod, then sat up straighter in his seat, his gaze sweeping the snow-covered landscape on the left side of the road. ''We're getting close.''

Theresa dropped her hand from his arm, adrenaline shooting through her. Eric. Eric. Her heart thundered his name as she prayed that they'd find him alive.

She knew it was possible they were on a wild-goose chase, that they'd get out to the farmhouse and find nothing. It was possible that Donny was keeping Eric someplace else.

''Theresa, get in the glove box and hand me my gun,'' Sully instructed as he turned off the highway onto a long driveway.

She opened the glove box, and as she wrapped her fingers around the butt of the gun, the danger of the situation became horrifyingly real.

If Sully's memories were true, then Donny had already attempted cold-blooded murder once. He'd proved himself to be an evil man with no conscience. He wouldn't give himself up easily, and Theresa was suddenly afraid not only for her son, but for Sully, as well.

Sully took the gun from her, then pointed up ahead, where a farmhouse had come into view. The two-story house looked forbidding, with its faded, peeling paint and broken windows. A thick copse of woods provided a dismal background, accentuating the feeling of isolation and abandonment.

As Sully pulled the car up front, Donny's distinctive yellow Corvette came into view, parked against the side of the house. "He won't be going anywhere too soon in that car, with this weather," Sully said, his voice tight with emotion. "You stay here in the car. I'm going to look around."

His voice left no room for argument. He turned off the car engine, flipped the safety off his gun and got out of the car.

"Sully?"

He bent down and looked at her.

"Be careful."

He nodded, for a moment his gaze caressing her face, as if he were memorizing her features. He straightened and closed the door.

Theresa watched him make his way to the house, holding her breath as he disappeared inside. She wrapped her arms around herself, drawing deep breaths to calm her racing heart.

A minute passed. Two minutes. What was happening? Where was Sully? Three minutes. Four minutes. Had he found Eric? Had he encountered Donny? What was taking so long? What was happening?

She gasped in relief when he appeared once again in the front doorway. He came down the stairs, indicating to her that he'd found nothing. Bitter disappointment rose in the back of her throat.

The snow had stopped for the moment, and she watched as Sully walked around Donny's car, then toward the woods. She could stand it no longer. She needed to be a part of this, to help him look for their son. Two could look faster than one.

She got out of the car, the cold wind stealing her breath away. Pulling her coat more firmly around her, she decided to go around to the back of the house in the opposite direction from the one Sully had taken.

The snow crunched beneath her feet, piercing the strange, almost otherworldly silence that snow always seemed to bring. She tried not to think of Eric being out in this weather, without boots, without gloves.

It was funny—she wanted to pray that Eric didn't feel the cold, but was afraid God would take her plea too seriously and her little boy would be beyond pain and cold. Funny and horrifying.

Her heart quickened when she saw the slanting door of a storm cellar. Although no footprints marred the snow surrounding the door, Theresa knew that with the way the wind was blowing, footprints would disappear quickly.

Knowing she should probably wait for Sully, yet too impatient to do so, she leaned down and pulled the door open. It creaked in protest, but opened to display a set of stairs that led down to a concrete floor.

Theresa listened for a moment, trying to hear any indication of life. Nothing. No sound at all drifted up the stairs. She went down one step, closing her eyes for a moment and sending a prayer upward. Please...please don't let me find his body. Surely the Fates wouldn't be so cruel.

She took another step down. *It's Christmas. Please give me back my baby, let him be alive and well. Don't let him be in this dank, dreary cellar. Don't let this horrid place be the last thing he saw.*

She nearly ran down the last several steps, stopped at the bottom and gasped when she saw the bare mattress, the portable toilet...the comic books and food wrappers that were evidence that somebody had spent time down here.

Eric. She knew he'd been here. She smelled him in the air, like an animal identifying her young. She knew his scent, and it was his boyish odor that surrounded her. She drew in deeply, wanting to capture the air that breathed of him, hold it in her lungs until she could hold him in her arms.

As she picked up one of the comic books, her stomach ached with a visceral pain. She could almost feel the warmth of his fingers on the pages.

She dropped the book and looked around, her heart aching as she thought of him trapped down here, without heat, without hope. Without his mom and dad to help him through the dark nights. Tears fell, one after another, choking her, strangling her.

He'd been here. But he wasn't here now. Where was he? Were they too late? Oh, God, were they too late? She sank to her knees, once again grabbing one of the comic books and clutching it to her chest.

Through her tears, she looked at the window, trying to imagine Eric looking out, waiting for her and Sully to find him, praying they got to him in time. She frowned, noticing the boards on the floor. Boards that appeared to have been across the window.

She stood and walked over to the window, where small shards of glass glittered on the snow outside. Outside. The window had been broken from the inside out. Her heart leaped when she saw a red thread stuck to part of the window frame.

Red. Eric's jacket. He'd crawled out. A sob escaped her and broke the inertia grief had spun within her. Eric had gotten out. He'd escaped from this hellhole. She stared out the window, toward the dense woods in the distance. "Eric?" she whispered, then raced up the stairs to find Sully.

SULLY had never been so cold in his life, and he knew the chill that gripped him had nothing to do with the snow or the temperature.

As he crept toward the woods, seeking Donny and answers, he knew he was about to step into the very fabric of his doubts, his nightmares. And with a misstep, with a single hesitation, it would no longer be Louie Albright's life on his conscience, but his own son's.

He felt like a hunter, seeking the deadliest of prey. Man. He tightened his grip around the butt of the gun, wondering, if and when the time came, whether he could pull the trigger, or whether he'd freeze, just as in his dreams.

He froze as Donny stepped out of the woods. Donny, instantly seeing him, halted for just a split second. "Hey, Sully." A smile curved his lips upward. "What are you doing out here? Gosh, am I glad to see you. I came out to do a little work around the place and got caught with the weather."

"Cut the crap, Donny." The words exploded from Sully with the velocity of bullets as he aimed his gun at the man who'd been his partner, his brother.

"Sully, what's the matter with you, man? What's going on here?"

Oh, he's good, Sully thought. He's so damned good. It appeared to be genuine bewilderment on his features. Donny held his hands out beseechingly. "Hey, man, put the gun down. Tell me what's going on here."

"Where's my kid? Where's Eric?"

Donny's eyes widened. "Sully, what in the hell are you talking about?"

For just a moment, doubts filtered through Sully. Was it possible Kip was right, that Donny was a dirty cop, but not responsible for Eric's kidnapping?

"Hey, come on. Talk to me." Donny took a step forward.

"Don't move, Donny. I'm feeling very upset, and I'd hate to do something you'll regret." The butt of the gun felt slippery from Sully's perspiration. He wondered if he could shoot Donny. Wondered if he still had what it took to pull the trigger. "I remember, Donny. You were there...the night I was shot."

"My God, Sully, what are you talking about? You've lost it, man. Remember, I was home sick with the flu."

"They kept the bullet, Donny. I wonder if a match could be made with your gun. The lab never found a gun to match it with. We never thought about checking your gun."

The confidence in Donny's eyes receded, and cold hatred took its place. "You know how sick I was of being your partner? The great Sullivan Mathews and his partner, what's-his-name." Sully felt the force of Donny's malevolence, as if it were a living, breathing force from him. "Yeah...I was there that night. I set it up with Louie, told him I was going to play a joke on you. But the joke was on Louie...and on me, because you didn't die."

A soul-sickness swept through Sully. "You tried to kill me because I got more press than you?" Sully asked incredulously.

"You got all of it!" Donny screamed, his features now twisted with the madness that had been hidden beneath the surface. "I was never going to get anywhere as long as you were around. Your shadow was too big, Sully...too deep. You had to go."

"You bastard." Theresa appeared from around the side of the house and ran toward them, tears streaming down her face. "You bastard. He trusted you. You were his partner."

Sully's heart skipped a beat as he realized that Theresa's tears, her emotion, were for him. After all he'd done to her, even though he had walked out on her, her hurt was for him. At the same time Theresa yelled, Donny pulled his gun and fired.

"Get down!" Sully screamed to Theresa as he hit the ground and rolled. Donny disappeared behind a tree. Seeing that Theresa had taken refuge at the back of Donny's car, Sully continued to roll until he had the cover of a thick tree trunk.

"Go home, Sully." Donny's voice eddied in the air, echoing in the natural acoustics the woods created. "Nobody is going to believe anything you say about me. Everyone knows you're nothing but a drunk, a has-been."

The wail of sirens sounded somewhere in the distance. Kip, Sully thought. Kip, coming with backup.

"Where's my son?" Theresa screamed.

"I don't know, Theresa," Donny answered. "Your husband is crazy. He needs help."

Hatred blinded Sully. He heard the sound of Theresa crying, and he hated Donny for hurting her, hated him for causing Sully a moment of self-doubt. "Hear the sirens, Donny? Your brothers are coming for you. Make it easier on yourself, tell me where Eric is."

"Go to hell, Sully." Donny punctuated his sentence by firing a shot. The bullet dug into the tree, sending wood chips across Sully's face.

Sully knew then that he would not hesitate to kill Donny Holbrook. His nightmare of freezing no longer held any power over him. If he had a clear shot, there would be no hesitation. Except...except a dead Donny couldn't tell them where Eric was. A dead Donny would take Eric's location with him to hell.

Sully wanted to laugh at the perversity of it all. For eighteen months he'd been afraid that he'd freeze, be unable to shoot when it became necessary. Now that he knew he could...he couldn't.

The sirens grew louder, closer, and in the distance Sully could see a parade of flashing lights coming up the drive.

Apparently, Donny saw them, too, knew his time was running out. Firing a succession of shots, he turned and raced deeper into the woods.

Without hesitation, Sully ran after him, knowing that if Donny managed to evade them, they might never know what happened to Eric.

"SULLY!" Theresa screamed as the two men disappeared into the thick woods. She leaned weakly against the fender of the sports car, fear making it impossible for her to stand on her own.

She'd heard the hatred spewing from Donny, and

she knew now that the man was truly mad. Where was Eric? Dear God, what had he done to Eric?

It had begun to snow again...small, wet flakes like frozen teardrops. Theresa stared toward the woods, the snow making it difficult to see.

As the police cars pulled up behind Donny's car, a gunshot splintered the air. "Sully!" Theresa screamed again and took off running in the direction of the woods.

Kip grabbed her by the arm. "Stay here," he commanded, and then he and half a dozen other officers ran toward the woods.

Theresa walked back to Donny's car, knowing there was nothing she could do but wait...and hope...and pray. She closed her eyes and heard the sounds of the officers shouting orders.

She tried to hear Sully's voice in the din, prayed that Donny hadn't managed to do what he'd tried to do in that alley. Keeping her gaze focused on the woods, she prayed for Sully's safety, for Eric's return.

After what seemed an eternity, men started coming out of the woods. First two policemen, their navy coats dark against the whitened landscape. Behind them, two more cops flanked Donny, who was in handcuffs. Where was Sully?

Her breath came fast, so fast she felt dizzy, as if not enough oxygen were getting to her brain. Where was Sully?

She gasped in relief when she finally saw him, walking tall and unharmed from the woods. Kip and two other officers were with him, but there was no sign of Eric.

"Donny, where's Eric?" Sully asked as he approached the handcuffed man.

"For God's sakes, Donny, tell them where their boy is," Kip added, his disgust for his fellow officer apparent.

Donny's eyes burned with a feverish light, his madness no longer hidden, but there for all to see. He laughed and shook his head, as if their pain were a joy, their torment a delight.

"I saw the cellar, Donny," Theresa said. "I saw where you kept him. It's over now. Tell us where he is."

"He wasn't supposed to get out. I was just going to keep him here for a couple of days, then bring him back to you and be a hero."

Theresa gasped at his admission, appalled by the fact that her son had been a pawn in a twisted plot to make Donny a hero.

"They would have made me chief for sure," Donny continued. "I was going to bring him back to you, and nobody would know the difference. But he saw me. The brat climbed out of the window and saw my face. So I had to kill him."

"No." The single word escaped from Theresa like the moan of the wind. She was vaguely aware of Sully, being held by Kip and another man, as he struggled to get to Donny.

"You want to know where your son is?" Donny's

eyes glittered with hatred. "He's there." He pointed to the woods. "Buried under the snow."

"No!" Theresa screamed and fell to her knees in the snow, her world shattering into a million pieces as the snow continued to fall.

Chapter Fifteen

Sully watched, heart dead, as the two officers placed Donny in the back of one of the patrol cars, then slowly drove down the long drive. The red and blue lights on top of the patrol car receeded in the distance, until they could no longer be seen amid the white, thick spill of snow from the skies.

"I'll put in a call for the dogs and a search team," Kip said as he laid a hand on Sully's shoulder. "God, Sully. I'm sorry. I'm so sorry." His face was twisted with sympathy.

Sully nodded—empty, hollow, inside. He knew eventually he'd cry for Eric, but at the moment he was numb.

It was too much to bear. It was all just too much to bear. That Eric had died because of a man's ambition. That they'd all been too late to save him.

He turned as Theresa picked herself up from the ground. Her eyes were as dull and dead as his. Slowly, as if sleepwalking, she moved to a pile of cut firewood and picked up a long, thick piece of wood. Before Sully could guess her intent, she swung the club and slammed it onto the hood of Donny's car, the fiberglass instantly cracking beneath the blow.

Kip turned, moved to go stop her, but Sully laid a hand on his arm. "Don't," he commanded.

Sully watched as she swung the piece of wood again and again, sobbing as she shattered the front windshield, then the back one. Like a woman possessed, she beat the car again and again as her sobs became screams of despair.

"Sully...maybe you should stop her," Kip said.

Sully turned and looked at his friend. "No. Leave her alone. She needs to do this." Kip nodded, and Sully turned back to watch Theresa vent her grief.

It didn't take long for her to run out of steam. She finally dropped the piece of wood as her tears stopped. She looked up at Sully, walked toward him, into his arms.

He held her tight, tighter than he had in his life, wishing he could take away her hurt, but he couldn't, because he was filled with the same hurt. There was no way to make this better, no way to minimize their loss. Nothing would ever make sense in their life again.

It was a long time before she finally stirred from his arms. "What do we do now? How do we go on?" she asked, her voice as dead as Sully felt.

He had no answer for her, knew she really didn't expect any. There was a hole in their lives now, a hole that would never be filled, a wound that would never, ever heal. Forever, their lives would hold sorrow of the deepest kind.

She moved away from him and started walking toward the woods. "Theresa...wait. What are you doing?"

She turned back to look at him, her blue eyes filled with anguish. "We have to find him, Sully. We can't let him stay out there all alone. You know he's scared of the dark."

Her words were a knife twisting in Sully's gut. "Kip has a search team coming. They'll find him, Theresa. We won't leave here without him. I promise."

She nodded, tears once again filling her eyes. "Oh, Sully."

Once again he wrapped her in his arms, knowing there was nothing left to comfort either of them, except the knowledge that they'd both loved him more than life itself.

"Hey, Sully!" Kip yelled to him from his patrol car.

Sully ignored him, focusing his full attention on the woman who shivered in his arms, the woman who'd carried Eric for nine months before Sully even knew the child. How would they go on without the little boy who'd brought such joy, such love, to their lives?

"Hey, Sully." Kip's voice intruded once again, filled with a strange excitement. "Headquarters just got a call from a gas station about a mile down Highway 10. A little boy just walked in...says his name is Joe Montana."

Sully stiffened in shock as Theresa gasped. "It's him," she said. "I know it's Eric." She laughed, tears racing down her cheeks. "He lied. Dear God, Donny lied when he said he'd killed Eric."

As if on cue, acting on a single thought, Sully and Theresa ran for Sully's car. Within minutes, Sully was driving down the snow-laden lane, heading for Highway 10 and Eric.

Theresa sat forward, straining against her seat belt as if by sheer will alone she could force the car to go faster. Sully felt almost dizzy from the roller-coaster emotions he'd experienced in the past few minutes. From utter despair to wondrous joy.

There was no way the boy could not be Eric. Anything else would be coincidental beyond belief. "I knew if there was a way to escape, he would."

Theresa flashed him a brilliant smile. "He's like his father, brave and smart."

Sully tried to return her smile, but he couldn't. He wasn't brave, or smart. If he was brave, he would have faced that alley months ago, forced himself to discover the dark secret his mind retained. If he was smart, he would have figured out Donny's part in this long before he did.

"There!" Theresa cried, pointing ahead, to the gas station's flickering neon sign.

Sully stepped on the gas, skidding into the parking lot and just barely missing the pumps. Before he could come to a complete halt, Theresa had unbuckled her seat belt and jumped out of the car. "Eric?" he heard her cry, and then Eric was there, standing in the doorway of the gas station.

At the sight of his little boy, with his big smile, face dirty, coat torn, Sully threw the car into park and burst into tears. Gulping sobs of relief tore through his chest as he watched Theresa embrace the child of his heart.

He gave her a moment alone, allowing her time to check Eric's arms, his legs, a mother hen seeing to her chick's well-being. She hugged him again and again, laughing and crying at the same time.

Finally, Sully's tears eased, the pressure in his chest receded, and he got out of the car. Theresa released Eric, and the little boy grinned at his father. "Hi, Dad." He lifted a hand in greeting. "I knew you'd come. I knew you'd find me."

In three long strides, Sully reached his son and grabbed him up in his arms. Closing his eyes, he squeezed Eric tight, breathing in the scent of him, reveling in the feel of Eric's sturdy body in his arms. "We missed you, son."

"I missed you, too, Dad." Eric placed a palm against Sully's cheek. "I wasn't scared...at least not so much. I knew you'd find me, Dad, 'cause you're a hero and that's what heroes do."

A sob caught in Sully's throat. Oh, how this child awed and amazed him. With his utter belief in heroes and his utter belief in Sully.

"Can we go home now? I'm starving," Eric said.

Sully laughed, his laughter ringing with Theresa's.

The resilience of children. "Yes, we can go home now." Together, the three of them headed for the car.

THERESA SAT ON THE SOFA, her eyes shining as she looked at the Christmas tree, now complete, the heavenly angel smiling down from the highest point. They'd decided to have their Christmas celebration the next morning, after Eric got a good night's sleep.

The afternoon had passed in a flurry of activity. While Eric had bathed, Theresa had fixed them all soup and grilled cheese sandwiches. As they ate, he'd told them about his time in that little cell, the picture he'd painted in his mind to keep fear away. He told them about running through the woods, Donny following. He'd hidden, the blowing wind helping his escape by instantly covering his tracks.

And now her son was tucked in bed, his new dog at his side and his father sitting in the chair next to him.

She smiled as she remembered Eric's joy when Montana had greeted them at the door. "He's mine? He's really, really mine?" Eric had asked, his eyes shining with excitement. It had been a case of instant mutual love between boy and dog.

She looked up and smiled as Sully came out of Eric's room and into the living room. She patted the sofa next to her. "Is he asleep?"

Sully nodded and sank down on the sofa. "Do you have any idea how lucky we are?"

She smiled. "I've just been sitting here counting

my blessings.'' Her smile fell as a shiver walked up her spine. ''I thought we'd lost him, Sully.''

Sully's mouth pressed into a thin line. ''That's exactly what Donny wanted us to think.'' He looked at Theresa, his gray eyes still holding the shadows of the experience. Theresa knew it would be some time before they healed, before they could put this all behind them.

He leaned back against the sofa and raked a hand through his hair. ''Imagine, orchestrating a kidnapping for ambition, to get your name in the paper.''

''He's sick, Sully. Donny is sick.''

He shook his head thoughtfully. ''I know, but I keep thinking somehow I should have seen some sign, I should have known something was going on inside him. We worked together for long hours, ate together and talked. Why didn't I see it?''

''Sully, give yourself a break. Donny was good. He had two faces, one a normal, rational one that he showed to the world, and a dark, twisted one that nobody saw.''

''I could kill him,'' Sully said, his voice tense with emotion.

''I killed his car.''

Sully looked at her, a slow smile curving his lips. ''You creamed it,'' he agreed.

Suddenly, they were laughing. Gales of laughter bubbled from them as they fell together, clinging to one another. In some distant space in her mind, Theresa knew it wasn't funny. And yet she surrendered to it, feeling the healing magic the shared laughter contained.

As she fell against Sully's chest, slid her arms around his neck, the rumble of his laughter filled her heart and she knew she'd never love another man the way she loved this man.

Her laughter faded, as did his, as she placed her head on his chest, heard the comforting sound of his heartbeat.

"If I had my way, I'd never let you or Eric out of my sight again," she said softly.

He stroked a hand through her hair. "But you know that's not only impossible, it's unhealthy. It's important that you don't smother Eric, overcompensate by taking away his independence."

"I know." Theresa knew she should sit up, pull herself away from the comfort of Sully's arms, but she didn't want to. It didn't seem fair that when she had Eric, she hadn't had Sully, and now that she had Eric home safe once again, she knew it was just a matter of time before Sully was gone again.

For a long moment, they remained there, with the light from the tree splashing merry colors all around them. Sully's hand was gentle as he stroked through her hair, and his heartbeat remained strong and vital in her ear.

It wasn't until Theresa began to caress the breadth of his chest that his heartbeat quickened and he stirred from their position.

"I need to be getting home," he said.

Theresa sighed as he said the words she'd been

dreading. She sat up and looked at him, loving the gray eyes, with their dark framing lashes and solemn light. In the space of three terror-filled days, he'd reentered her heart so completely, filled the empty spaces she hadn't realized existed inside her.

A year ago, when he walked away from their marriage, she'd let him go without a whimper, because she believed him so unhappy with her. This time, she said the words she hadn't been able to say before. "Sully...don't go."

"I'll be back in the morning for the Christmas celebration," he said as he averted his gaze from her. She had a feeling he was deliberately misunderstanding what she wanted. He stood and looked at the angel on top of the tree. "Eric's home safe, the angel is where she belongs, and it's time for me to go home."

In the past three days, Theresa had faced the worst that life could offer, and she'd had to realize how brief, how fragile, life and happiness could be. As she looked up at Sully, the man she loved, the man she would always love, she realized that this time she wasn't going to let him go without a fight. Pride be damned, life was too short for her to watch her happiness walk out her front door.

If he could convince her that he no longer loved her, that he'd left her before because he was unhappy with her, then she'd have to let him go. But as she thought back over the past three days, remembered the way Sully had touched her, the way his eyes had sparked with desire, she simply couldn't believe he no longer loved her.

She stood and walked toward him. "Sully, I don't want you to go, not tonight. Not ever."

His face twisted, as if her words pained him. It was a pain she couldn't understand. "Theresa, you're allowing the emotions and what we've been through to—"

"Dammit, Sully, stop it right now," she said, her voice low with anger. "Stop telling me what I think and what I feel. This has nothing to do with Eric's abduction, this has nothing to do with the past three days. I love you. I never stopped loving you, and I want us to be a family again...the three of us."

"I can't do that. You just don't understand."

"Then make me understand." She grabbed his hands in hers, held them tight when he tried to pull away. "You still love me, Sully. You can't deny it. And I love you. So tell me what I don't understand. Talk to me, Sully," she begged. "You didn't talk to me after you got shot. Dear God, please talk to me now."

His gaze held hers for a long, unguarded moment and in his eyes she saw his love for her, knew she'd been right. He loved her. Sully loved her. Her heart sang with the knowledge.

The joy was short-lived. Almost gently, he eased his hands away from hers and stepped back, deep shadows obscuring the love she'd seen moments before, shining in his eyes. "You're right. I owe you some answers."

He swiped a hand through his dark hair, then turned away from her, as if unable to speak and look at her at the same time. "You've always been the strongest woman I know, Theresa. It was one of the things I admired about you. When I'd go off to do my job as a cop, you never clung to me, never demanded of me." He turned and looked at her once again. "I watched you prosecute the worst kind of criminals, saw you look them in the face without fear. I watched you bury your mother and saw the strength you used to help your sisters with their grief."

"What does any of this have to do with us?" she asked impatiently.

"Because I can't live up to being the man you deserve." His voice was so filled with bitterness, with regret, her heart ached. "Because for the last eighteen months I've been afraid." His eyes darkened to the deep shadows of night. "Afraid, Theresa...like a child. I tried booze to quiet the fear, but that didn't work. I needed to leave you before you grew to hate me, before you realized what a scared, weak fool I was."

"Oh, Sully." She reached for him, but he drew away from her.

"I watched my mother grow to hate my father. I never wanted that to happen to us. I figured it was better you hate me for leaving than hate me for being weak."

Theresa sank down onto the sofa, realizing there was a lot of baggage between them. "Tell me, Sully.

Tell me about that night. Tell me all the ugly, horrid things you didn't want to tell me before.'' Somehow, she felt the answer was there...in the events of that night. The answer to why Sully had started hating himself so much he couldn't accept that she loved him, didn't feel worthy of that love.

''You really want to hear about it?'' His dark eyes held a hint of anger...anger Theresa knew wasn't directed at her, but rather was directed inward.

''As I walked toward the alley, I saw Donny's car, but somehow it didn't register in my head that it shouldn't be there, was out of place.'' Sully began to pace back and forth in front of her. His voice low and steady, as if he were reciting something that had happened not to him, but to somebody else. ''But I knew something wasn't right, had a bad feeling in my gut. Still, that didn't stop me. I got to Louie at the end of the alley, and we said a few things. Then I heard it...the metallic click of a gun being cocked, and I froze.''

He stopped pacing and stared at her, his eyes dead and empty. ''I froze,'' he repeated. ''Then Louie was dead, and I thought I was, too.'' He drew in a deep, shuddering breath. ''I might have been able to save Louie if I hadn't frozen with fear. Don't you see, his death is as much my fault as it is Donny's. If I hadn't been such a coward, if fear hadn't frozen me to the spot, Louie wouldn't be dead.''

Theresa sucked in air, realized that this was what had taken Sully away from her. A death he felt responsible for, a life he thought was gone because he hadn't reacted appropriately. Tears glittered on his eyelashes, attesting to the weight of this burden, a burden that had stolen his self-esteem, imbued him with a self-hatred that was destroying him.

"How long do you suppose it takes between the cocking of a gun and the pulling of the trigger?" she asked.

"What?" He stared at her blankly, as if she'd suddenly spoken a foreign language.

"Oh, Sullivan, we've got to do something about this penchant you have for carrying the weight of the world on your back." She stood and walked toward him. "I said, how long does it take between cocking a gun and the bullet being discharged?"

"I don't know.... A second." He continued to stare at her, comprehension lightening the shadows of his eyes. "A second at the most."

"You froze for a second, Sully. What could you have done in that space of time to save Louie? Save yourself?"

"Nothing." The word seeped from him hoarsely. "In my nightmares, that moment always seems so agonizingly long. I just stand there for what seems like minutes, and then Louie is dead."

"But it couldn't have been minutes." Theresa placed her palm on the side of his face. "Sully, you're no more responsible for Louie's death than you are Eric's kidnapping." She placed her other hand on his cheek, capturing the face she loved between her hands. "And if you hadn't been afraid, then you wouldn't have been human."

"I didn't want you to know my weaknesses," he admitted. "You never showed me any of yours."

She frowned. "I got used to hiding mine from my family. After Dad walked out on us, I knew I had to hold the family together, and if they saw me upset or afraid, then they would be upset or afraid. But, Sully, I was wrong to hide from you. We spent all our married life hiding our warts from each other. Can't we try it again, only this time share it all...the good and the bad?"

"Oh, Theresa, I love you so much. I just wanted to always be your hero."

His words renewed the joy in her heart as his lips captured hers in a kiss of such love, of simmering desire and the promise of dreams yet to be fulfilled. She wound her arms around his neck, feeling as if fate had truly blessed her.

"Sully, you are my hero. It's because you were with me, beside me, that I could be strong. You, Sully, you were and are my strength," she said as his lips left hers.

He tightened his arms around her, pulling her so close she couldn't tell where she left off and he began. "I love you, Theresa. You and Eric, you're all that's good in my life."

She looked into his eyes, eyes no longer shadowed, no longer haunted. "Does this mean you'll stay with me? Stay forever?"

"Forever and a day," he replied, his eyes shining with the force of his love for her.

"Let's go wake up Eric, tell him he's getting his Christmas wish."

Sully tightened his arms around her. "Let's wait until morning," he said, his eyes sparking with a light of passion that stole Theresa's breath away.

As he swept her into his arms and carried her toward the bedroom, Theresa looked back at the angel on the tree. The angelic smile appearing bigger, brighter, than ever before.

Epilogue

Spring imbued the air with sweet fragrance and welcome warmth. For Theresa, winter had ended the day they found Eric alive and well, the night Sully came back to her. In actuality, winter had continued for two more months, but Theresa had hardly noticed.

She spread the blanket out on the ground, her diamond wedding ring catching the sun's rays and reflecting back sparkles. She straightened up and waved to Sully and Eric, who were playing catch in the distance. Montana ran between the two, barking each time they threw the ball.

Her gaze focused on Eric as his laughter rode the breeze. He'd suffered few residual effects from his traumatic experience. She guessed that much of his adjustment had come from Sully, who'd talked to his son about sick people and told the boy it was okay if he'd been afraid.

Her gaze moved to Sully. Her husband. They'd married two weeks after Eric was found. Eric had served as best man, and Montana had spent the entire ceremony trying to eat her bouquet.

He had returned to the police department, was once again doing what he loved. And once again he walked with pride, the shadows of that distant night no longer haunting him.

Marriage to him was different this time. Better. There were no secrets, no need to be perfect for one another. They shared a new bond, one forged in love and commitment and deepened by their faults and weaknesses.

But today she did have a secret. One that filled her heart with joy, one she couldn't wait to share with her family.

Hurriedly, eager to spill her news, she unpacked the picnic basket, then motioned her men to the blanket. "Oh, boy, I'm starving," Eric said as he flopped down and eyed the spread Theresa had put out. "Hmm, fried chicken." He grabbed a plate and began to fill it.

"Aren't you eating?" Sully asked as he ladled a liberal helping of potato salad on his plate.

"Oh, yes, I'm eating." With a tiny smile, she pulled a jar of pickles from the basket. "Now, if only I had some ice cream."

Sully froze, his gaze holding hers intently. She nodded, and he dropped his plate and pulled her to him. "Really?"

She laughed and nodded again.

"What's going on?" Eric asked, looking at his parents as if they'd lost their minds. Montana didn't seem to care, as he ate the potato salad on the plate Sully had dropped.

"You're going to have a little baby brother or sister," Theresa said to Eric.

Eric's eyes widened. "For real?"

"For real." Theresa smiled into Sully's eyes, eyes that held the wonder, the joy, she'd expected.

"That's awesome!" Eric exclaimed.

"Totally awesome," Sully agreed.

"I hope it's a boy. And I'll be a big brother." Eric's chest puffed out at the thought. "And I'll take care of him and make sure he never gets in trouble. I'll kind of be like you are to me, Dad."

Sully frowned. "What do you mean, son?"

"You know, I'll be his hero," Eric announced proudly.

Theresa saw the tears of joy that sparkled in Sully's eyes as he busied himself getting another plate. In those simple, innocent words, Eric had given Sully more than Eric would ever know.

Joe Montana had nothing on Sullivan Mathews. And Theresa had Sullivan Mathews for the rest of her life. And Eric. And a baby growing within her. And a dog who loved potato salad. She laughed with delight. She was one lucky woman.

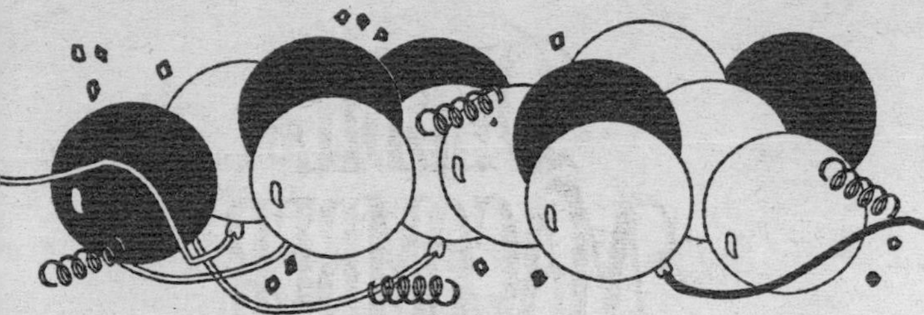

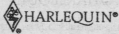

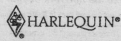